ZVI
AND THE NEXT GENERATION

ZVI
AND THE NEXT GENERATION

Copyright 1988
The Friends of Israel Gospel Ministry, Inc.
Bellmawr, New Jersey 08031

First Edition — 1988

Cover design: Barbara Alber and Tom Allen
Cover photograph: Shirley Glazier — Sunrise over the Sea of Galilee

Printed in the United States of America
Library of Congress Catalog Number 88-80875
ISBN 0-915540-43-6

ZVI
AND THE NEXT GENERATION

by
Elwood McQuaid

**THE FRIENDS OF ISRAEL
GOSPEL MINISTRY, INC.**
Bellmawr, New Jersey

*And he brought him forth abroad, and said,
Look now toward heaven, and count the stars,
if thou be able to number them: and he said
unto him, So shall thy seed be.*

Genesis 15:5

TABLE OF CONTENTS

INTRODUCTION

This book is a promise kept: First, to myself, and then to Zvi, Marv Rosenthal and the many hundreds of you who have asked the question over the last few years: "When will the sequel to ZVI be written?"

Well, here it is, and with a confession. When Marv Rosenthal suggested that we undertake this inevitable project, my first thought was: "But how can we do anything that will compare to the sheer wonder inspired by the miraculous story of Zvi's early life?"

But as I got into the project, I quickly realized that we had something here which goes far beyond the thrilling scenes of the first book. ZVI AND THE NEXT GENERATION demonstrates in a very powerful way what can be expected from a faithful God who saved a youth, yes, but only as a first thread in a magnificent divine pattern.

As you follow the development of the larger circles of Zvi's life and witness, no doubt you will, as I have, raise expressions of gratitude to Him who puts His mark on us so that we, in turn, can be instruments through which He can mark many more for eternity. ZVI AND THE NEXT GENERATION shows us that pattern to perfection.

Allow me to recommend to those of you who haven't read ZVI to do it without fail. It is not a prerequisite for reading ZVI AND THE NEXT GENERATION, but it will certainly enrich your understanding of these later events.

Elwood Mc Quaid

CHAPTER ONE

D. O. A.

His expressionless face brought a sickening thump to their stomachs. It looked as though he wore a pale death mask. The characteristic animation that had made his eyes dance as facial creases bowed upward in laughter was gone — from all appearances, Zvi Weichert was dead!

They had found him face down at a bus stop on Jaffa Road in Jerusalem. Bystanders shook their heads as ambulance attendants tried to pound life back into his motionless chest. Finally, the heart began to flutter tentatively. The piercing wail of the ambulance siren signaled the start of the race for Zvi's life.

Shortly after his arrival at the hospital, the heart said "No" again.

"I'm sorry to have to tell you this," the hospital's chief cardiologist informed Esther, Zvi's wife, "but your husband is clinically dead. We've managed to get his heart going again, but we are convinced there is no hope for him. If we remove the life support system, his body will cease functioning immediately.

"Even if, by some miracle, he should regain consciousness, he can never be normal again. You see, his brain has been denied oxygen for too long during the periods of cardiac arrest.

"We've done all we can for him. It's only a matter of time. You had better get the family together."

Word got around the city quickly. The man who had eluded death with the agility of "a cat on the wall" was fresh out of lives.

Esther and the children — Mendel from work; Yona and Eli from the service; Ruth and her husband, David, from Eilat — sat in the small waiting room of the hospital and shared their tears.

Esther's face wore a worried expression as she began issuing directives. Zvi's children were accustomed to worried looks from their mother. As a matter of fact, she seemed to do all the worrying for the Weichert family. Their father didn't have the capacity to worry, at least where it showed. And if they had heard it once, they had heard it from him a thousand times: "So, OK! Don't worry. What will be, will be."

They wouldn't follow abba's advice today — today they would worry.

"Children," Esther began, "we don't know how long we will be here. You must remember to eat and keep up your strength. You may not feel like it now, but you must do as I tell you.

"Yona, call people from the church. Ask them to pray for your father. Mendel, call Marvin in America. Tell him what has happened and ask him to have believers there pray."

Ruth had been praying hard already. On the four-hour trip up from Eilat, she had scarcely noticed the barren landscape rushing past the car window. Her thoughts were absorbed by abba.

"It just isn't fair," she told herself. "All my father has known is war, sacrifice and doing for other people. He's only 58. He deserves some good years for himself."

Her emotions built until, in an intemperate surge of audacity, she flung a command heavenward, "My father cannot die!" she cried. "He must have another chance to live!" Later, when she had some time to think about it, Ruth would realize that God had been very patient with an overwrought child. But at that moment, her only priority was her father's life.

From a human point of view, it did seem grossly unfair. The window through which he had looked at life had, much too often, presented vistas of cruelty, suffering and death.

He was ten-year-old Henryk of Warsaw, Poland, when trouble first goose stepped its way into his small world. The Nazis had entered Warsaw with a summary execution notice for all Jews in Poland. It would take some doing, but Hitler was convinced he had crafted a "final solution to the Jewish problem" — kill them all! Before World War II began, some 3.3 million Jews lived in Poland. By the time the flames engulfed Hitler's body outside the bunker in Berlin, barely 300,000 Polish Jews could be accounted for — 3 million had been exterminated.

Hitler's "Final Solution" was planned to develop in three stages.

Isolation and intimidation began in 1939 when orders were issued to expel Jews from small towns and force them into the large cities where they could be concentrated in isolated areas.

Jews were systematically discriminated against through smaller food rations and being forbidden access to many areas in the cities. They were also subject to seizure for forced labor in German factories and installations.

This was the phase of the program which saw Henryk's brothers, Arthur, Hersh and Jacob, snatched from their home, never to be heard from again.

Violence and terror rained down on Polish Jews, who had been marked by orders that they wear identifying armbands and yellow stars of David which declared the wearer a Jew and, therefore, fair game for vicious diversions. Henryk's father was treated to scenes daily which would send him home sickened, depressed and silent. It was common to see S. S. troops howling in laughter around fallen elderly Jewish men as they took turns kicking their ribs in. Others roamed the streets with shears in hands to cut beards from religious Jews and force them into degrading acts. Jewish businesses smashed and looted, flames leaping into the sky from Warsaw's synagogues and Jews being randomly killed deepened Mendel's depression.

Phase two involved forcing *Jews to the ghettos*. In November of 1940, apprehensive Jewish residents of Warsaw watched as the bleak brick walls went up around the section to which they had been consigned — or condemned. Ghettoization meant cramming too many people into too little space. Disease and starvation would move in beside guns, clubs, fists and forced labor to help Hitler's program along. Mendel, Ruth and their daughter, Tema, were among those herded behind the wall to waste away among the sunken faces, death carts and joyless children.

By 1941, events had moved to the *extermination stage*. The infamous death camps were fully operational by this time and by September 1942, over 300,000 of Warsaw's Jews had made the journey from the ghetto to the death chambers at Treblinka.

Destroying the ghettos themselves was the final desecration — in some grotesque fashion it was like burning the mausoleum of those you've murdered. Determined resistance by Jewish remnants made the liquidators' work difficult. But, in the end, might prevailed, and by mid-May 1943, the Warsaw ghetto was no more. The winds fanning the dying fires of the ghetto carried away every sign of Mendel, Ruth and Tema. No trace of them would ever be found.

The Weicherts, being Jewish, had represented some very small obstacles on the path to the Hitlerian utopia. Their graves, in the estimation of their assigned executioners, would mark six stepping stones toward the Reich "that would last a thousand years."

Before they were taken to the ghetto, Mendel and Ruth decided to take a stab at denying the butcher in Berlin at least one victim of his monstrous quest for a Jewless world. They knew their fate was sealed. And they would take daughter Tema to the infamous Warsaw ghetto with them.

But perhaps, they reasoned, little Henryk could have a chance to survive.

At least, they would give it a try. They would disguise his Jewish identity, put him in an orphanage, and pray that somehow he would make it through the Holocaust.

The parting with his mother was burned into his memory. Her round face, framed in golden hair, was a stark contrast to the harsh gray walls of the orphanage. Ruth's body was warm against his as she spoke the last words he would hear her say.

"Henryk, I want you to make me a promise, one that you must always carry with you: Do not tell anyone here that you are a Jew."

The bewildered boy wanted to know why. "Because they don't like Jews here. You must watch your words. Be careful what you say, and always remember what I've told you.

"My son, you must learn to be strong. From now on you are no longer my child — now you are a man!"

He stood at a window and watched her cross a cold courtyard and stride through the arched gate. For her, it represented the gateway to the high walled ghetto, Treblinka and, if she survived that long, standing naked in the gas chamber. For Henryk, it was the entrance to years of clawing his way through the rubble of war in pursuit of staying alive.

Henryk and his contemporary Polish *waifs of war* would become enduring legends for their tenacity and ingenuity in the precarious art of survival. A popular ghetto song memorialized these children:

Over the walls, through holes, and past the guard,
Through the wires, ruins, and fences,
Plucky, hungry, and determined,
I sneak through, dart like a cat.

With the closing of the orphanage, Henryk joined the child smugglers who nightly slipped through the sewer slime and up into the ghetto with lumpy sacks of potatoes on their backs. The boy had two things on his mind. Like all of the others, he wanted to sell his produce for the means to sustain himself. His obsession, however, was to search for his parents and sister. Instead, he saw only the pallid faces of starving Jews, some stretched out before the store fronts raising boney hands toward Heaven while imploring the Messiah to come and deliver them from their agony. Remnants of their forlorn entreaties survive:

Therefore we plead with You ever:
Now help us, Guardian of Israel,
Now take notice of our tears,
For still we do cry aloud, "Hear O Israel."
O, take notice, Guardian of the nation.

Show all the peoples that You are our God,
We have indeed none other, just You alone,
Whose name is One.

Strange words, these, from strange faces, Henryk thought as he hurried down the streets looking for someone, anyone, who could give him some answers about his family. A familiar face finally turned up in Mordecai Friedman, a wealthy man from his old neighborhood, of whom he caught a glimpse as the old man walked slowly along the pavement. Their strange reunion — an old man absorbed in conversation with a small boy he had known but seldom noticed — produced counsel which, no doubt, contributed to the lad's survival.

"Henryk, let me give you some advice before we part. Don't spend too much time looking for them here. You are a boy and still strong. If you stay here in the ghetto, soon you will grow weak like the rest. Don't die here. Do everything you can to save yourself."

The boy heeded his elder's sage advice and launched out from Warsaw to seek haven and solve his hunger problems in the Polish countryside. Lice-filled barns, frozen fields, woods and a stint working for a Nazi loyalist, whose cruelty paralleled his revered Fuehrer's, filled his days before the war came to an end.

For the most part, the routine was suffering, pain, running for safety, beatings, anguish and bitter experiences. There were, however, a few welcomed islands of compassion and friendship which combined providentially to help bring him through.

There was a young Polish family who befriended him, got rid of the lice infesting his body, provided warm baths and a feeling of family and warmth around their table.

Nor would he ever forget the woman who invited him in after a numbing night on the frozen roads as he fled for his life. She fed him, put him in a clean, warm bed, allowed him a long, uninterrupted night's sleep, dressed him in dry clothing, and sent him away with a small bit of assurance that acts of human kindness had not passed completely off the face of the planet.

And when he had been beaten nearly to death by the Germans, after they caught him aiding the partisans, the doctor and nurse tending to his wounds and caring for him literally saved his life. His permanent scars were enduring reminders of the pleasant days spent recuperating under their watchful and compassionate eyes.

The face emerging from the mists of his mind most often, however, was that of Saul — a Jewish boy he befriended after he left Warsaw for the more productive fields surrounding farms in the country. Henryk's

17

compassion for Saul Blum ran deep almost from the instant the boy first caught his eye. This was probably because the malnourished kid from the Lodz ghetto wore all his own troubles written across his face. It looked like the boy had "Jew" written across his forehead in indelible ink. Henryk was amazed that one who looked so Jewish could have survived for five minutes on the open road.

Their relationship was more father and son than it was boy with boy. Henryk found hiding places, foraged and spent hours counseling his friend who had an irrepressible longing to rejoin his family in the ghetto at Lodz.

"Listen to me," Henryk cautioned, "we cannot act like blind fools. When I left the ghetto in Warsaw, I knew I must take my life in my own hands. If my parents are dead, I cannot help them by dying too. Neither can you. Your life is in your hands, and you must save it. Anyway, if you do succeed in getting into the ghetto, what is there for you then? A quick death at the hands of the Germans is better than slow starvation in the ghetto. If you want to die, go to a German and say, 'Look, I am a Jew. Take me and shoot me in the head.' "

His words fell on deaf ears. Before he ventured into the ghetto, Saul determined, he would snatch some coins from the money box of an old man who ran a store close to the ghetto. He wanted to take something to his starving family. It was a fatal decision.

Henryk watched in horror as he saw his friend running from the store directly into the path of a German soldier who was patrolling the streets. The German's words made him sick. "This little thief is a Jew! And we know what to do with Jew pigs."

Their friendship came to an abrupt end as Saul's writhing figure, held by the throat, was dragged backward up the street. The clatter of the coins falling from Saul's hands onto the pavement sounded the death knell for Henryk's boyhood and the nation he had loved as a child. The smell of death was all Poland meant to him.

The feeling persisted and became an entrenched conviction when the war ended and the search for his loved ones proved futile. All of Europe was as dead to Henryk as Saul and his family. He would seek his future, if indeed there was one, in a new place. That place would be Israel, land of the Jews. If he no longer had a family, at least he would be among his own people. There, perhaps, he would experience a new beginning.

But things in the Jewish "Promised Land" would begin much like they had ended in Hitler's Europe: more faces of death to remember. After a perilous journey across the Mediterranean and months of internment as an illegal immigrant on Cyprus, Henryk would find himself fighting for his life and that of reborn Israel in the 1948 War of Independence.

To the boys from Europe who were trained for the impending battles with Arab adversaries, this war seemed like a lark. They were supremely confident that the Arabs were no match for the likes of them — tough survivors of the Holocaust who had beaten Hitler at his deadly game.

"The Arabs will not like what we have for them," they laughed on the way to their first skirmish. "They will probably turn and run when they see us coming."

"If they don't, it will be their funeral," another said confidently.

The Arabs didn't turn and run — not at first. They fought, and Jewish boys quickly learned that bullets hit you just as hard in Israel as they had in Europe.

And in the heat-seared wheat fields around the village of Latrun, in the first significant battle of the war, Henryk would watch as more Jewish boys from Europe were systematically torn to shreds by Arab machine gunners. The dead ones wore a look of surprise, as if they could not comprehend, even in death, how they could survive the years in war-ravaged Europe to die within hours of their arrival in the place that was to be a safe haven for Jews.

Had he come here, he wondered, to once again play a deadly game of tag with death? Maybe he should surrender and see an end to it all. After all, perhaps his family and Saul were the lucky ones. Their suffering was over. His, it seemed, was only starting again.

But fortunately for Henryk, it was not the beginning of a drawn out and miserable end. It was the dawning of a new day, for when the war was over, both he and Israel were counted among the survivors.

The resilient orphan from Warsaw had a new land. He also had a new name — they called him Zvi. Zvi would shortly find a new life.

It came to him in a bag, carried down the rows of box-car-like barracks in Talpiyot (a transit camp on the Bethlehem side of Jerusalem) by a woman who invited him to take one of her little books.

"What kind of book is it?" he asked.

"This is a New Testament written in Hebrew," she answered cheerfully. "It will tell you about the Messiah."

"Yes," he told her, "I will be glad to read it."

"Read slowly and ask the Lord to lead you to understand what you read."

So Zvi read, and the Lord led. Soon he was consumed by a passion for the Book. He would take the New Testament with him into Jerusalem, find a quiet place and begin to read. On many occasions, when the light was gone, and he could no longer see the print, he would realize that he had been so absorbed by the Book he hadn't taken time to eat. And as the light began to break over his soul, he developed a deep desire to know the Christ of that precious Book.

He found Him in a small church on a quiet street in the Holy City. Pastor Moshe Kaplan explained the way of salvation.

Knowing the Lord, the pastor wanted Zvi to understand, was a serious matter. "Yes, I am aware of that," Zvi replied. "I have been thinking about it for a long time. Now I know it is what I have been searching for, but I did not know how to find it. I must find peace with God, and I know it can be found only through the Messiah."

"Here is a point you must understand," the pastor counseled, "if you accept Jesus as your Messiah and Savior, you will be in for trouble. It is very difficult for people to live openly for Christ here in Israel these days. It may be necessary for you to endure suffering if you become His follower."

Zvi understood.

"Good. Now the next question is this: Do you believe in Jesus as the Messiah and are you willing to accept Him as your Savior and Lord?"

"Yes — yes! Without any question," said Zvi. "I am convinced that He is the Messiah and my Savior."

With the transforming transaction he would come to know as the new birth, he found new life. To this point, Zvi's life had been nothing less than a miracle of survival against prohibitive odds. With his salvation, the Lord began working on a miracle of a far different kind.

1948 — 1967

CHAPTER TWO

THE NEXT GENERATION

T he victory of an infant nation, represented on the battlefield by thrown-together bands of youths who didn't even understand the language of their adopted land, must stand as one of the unique feats of war in mankind's history. Five Arab armies moved against them in a determined effort to hold back the tide of Jewish desire to return home created by the Holocaust and the United Nations' decision to resurrect Israel as a modern state. The sheer wonder of what was unfolding in the Middle East in 1948 stopped the world dead in its tracks and delivered a resounding affirmation of what some prophetic scholars had been saying all along: that a Jewish return to Palestine was inevitable.

Responsible conservative theologians saw it as a return to the land *in unbelief* in preparation for the climactic events of the last days and the consummating confrontation with the Messiah.

To Jewish minds, it was an entirely different matter. Nonreligious Zionists believed it was the fulfillment of the dream to forge a national Jewish homeland in the historical and cultural land of ancient Jewry — a place where Jewish will, dedication and ingenuity could give blood and bones to Herzl's words: "If you will it, it is no dream."

Some religious Zionists had another idea. This was the beginning of the end of the messianic vision. For millennia, they and their forebears had prayed and wept for the day when they could ascend the hills of Zion. Passover cups raised throughout the diaspora above the ubiquitous sentence "Next year in Jerusalem!" could now be put down on tables in Israel. They were living the dream that would bring Messiah to His Chosen People in His Promised Land.

There were those who disagreed. Elements of the Hasidic movement — ultra-Orthodox Jews — believed there could be no legitimate state of Israel before the Messiah comes. He alone can declare Israel a national, historical reality. They would have no part in a secular government — except, of course, accepting selected benefits.

In reality, their victory in the War of Independence was but the first phase of a series of highs and lows which were to mark the strategic transitional swings awaiting those first expectant citizens of the fledgling state.

Over the next forty years, Israelis were to experience at least three exhilarating highs.

The first was the birth of the state on May 15, 1948 and the subsequent survival of the nation against all odds.

But the religious and emotional high-water mark — even surpassing the first reality — was the reunification of Jerusalem on the morning of June 7, 1967. At long last there was substance to their song: "...to live in freedom in the land of Zion and *Jerusalem*."

The water began to recede on October 6, 1973. During the Yom Kippur War, Israel staggered along the brink of annihilation. It was a war which was a military victory, but an emotional loss. Much of the steam was taken out of the drive toward the Zionist ideal. Israel faced a long-term reality — staying alive in the Middle East among enemies set to destroy her and friends who seemed quick to sacrifice principle for petroleum and commitments for cash.

Optimism rose again when Anwar Sadat made his historic visit to Jerusalem in 1979. In the aftermath of that visit, Camp David in America seemed to offer some promise of peace for the sons of David in Israel. Perhaps, after all, accommodation could be reached and respite could come to a people tired of endless preparedness for war. It was a move which cost Sadat his life because Arab fanatics were infuriated over his making peace with Israel and feared they were in danger of losing their justification for spilling Jewish blood. It was a fear which spurred them to accelerate attempts to slaughter innocents in the spurious name of *the Palestinian cause*.

The most convenient and frequent object of their wrath was northern Israel. Terrorist activities there precipitated Israel's invasion of her northern neighbor's territory. It was something most agreed must be done, but the doing was distasteful business. Before it was over, Lebanon would breed internal dissent that would accentuate factional disputes already present inside Israel.

Internal strife would progressively become more pronounced and serve to fan the frustration, thereby creating a situation which resulted in uncharacteristicly violent acts by a small segment of Jews against Arabs and, in some cases, Jews against other Jews.

Tension between religious and nonreligious Israelis was continually rising as these other problems were buffeting the nation. Secular and less-religious Jews were increasingly fed up with the picayunish regulations imposed on their lives by a relatively small segment of ultra-Orthodox people. Their representatives in the Knesset perpetually held the government hostage, threatening to destroy the ruling coalition by walking out if they didn't get their way. Such intimidation often did get them their way and brought on even more unrest and dissention between the two communities.

Uprisings by Palestinians on the West Bank and in Gaza — acts orchestrated by Yassir Arafat and his cohorts — were aimed at destroying renewed attempts by Israelis and some legitimate Arab leaders to reach a settlement. Israel reacted resolutely, restrained the violence and restored order in the territories. The predictable condemnation by the United Nations and criticism by American officials of Israel's handling of the matter compounded the problems and further eroded morale among some segments of the population.

Inside Israel, there are those who liken developments to the internal situation just before the Roman conquest of Jerusalem in 70 A. D., when party was pitted against party, and infighting between competing interest groups destroyed national unity.

But while, over four decades, these events unfolded, a new generation of Israelis was coming onto the scene. In some ways, as is true the world over, they have brought significant problems in their baggage. But in spiritual matters, they are relatively free of some of the inhibiting concepts held by the last generation.

Above every other consideration, one can observe the hand of a sovereign God moving Israel toward a biblically revealed climax. At the same time, He is opening magnificent opportunities to enlarge the believing remnant among second generation Israelis. And, as we shall see, the Lord has been pleased to boldly weave the life and witness of Zvi and his *next generation* into this intriguing tapestry.

Israel's optimism following the War of Independence covered Zvi as it did the nation. Coming to know the Messiah had changed everything — he had something — better, Someone — to live for. Granted, he was still in the army and, as a sapper (an engineer who lays, detects and disarms mines), continued to practice the precarious occupation in which you couldn't

25

make the same mistake *once*. But now he knew his life was in the hands of the Lord, and whatever happened to him was the Father's concern. In the will of God, "what would be, would be," and it was OK with him.

Zvi completed his service as an army regular in 1950. But, as is true with all Israeli Defense Force conscripts, he owed his country another 33 years of his life as a reservist. Consequently, he was "on call" whenever trouble was afoot. And terrorist activity would keep him busy soldiering in the years between 1950 and 1956.

Agitation and unrest were rampant during these years as the Arabs, so decisively beaten in the War of Independence, tried to save face and recoup their losses. After the armistice was signed, Israel's Foreign Minister, Moshe Sharett, spoke prophetic words before the Knesset. "The storm which has been raging around us will not soon be stilled. Nor do we hold certainty in our hearts that it will not break out anew, with greater violence...." He was right on the mark.

Between 1950 and 1956, border violations by Arab infiltrators, mine laying on Israeli roads and tracks and armed incursions were almost daily occurrences. During that period, over 400 Israelis were killed and 900 injured. There were 3,000 armed clashes with Arab forces and at least 6,000 acts of sabotage.

Egypt's Gamal Abdel Nasser was a foremost perpetrator of this mischief, with Egyptian *fedayeen* (suicide fighters) acting as his primary agents. Zvi found himself almost constantly roving the roads and tracks, dislodging the mines the *fedayeen* and others were planting.

Things came to a head in 1956, after Egypt had closed the Suez Canal to shipping bound for Israel and pitched out the British as canal operators by nationalizing the waterway. In the minds of the British and French, this posed an unacceptable danger to shipping, and they collaborated with Israel to bring an end to Nasser's adventurism.

Israel's objectives were to destroy *fedayeen* bases in the Gaza Strip and on the Sinai border; preempt Egypt's ability to attack Israel by destroying fortifications and airfields in the Sinai; and open the Gulf of Eilat to undisturbed Israeli shipping. All of these objectives were accomplished.

The Sinai Campaign itself lasted less than eight days — from October 29 to November 5, 1956. Israel, Britain and France had secretly agreed to join forces in clearing the Sinai and securing the canal. The plan called for Israel to punch into the Sinai, after which France and Britain would land troops in order to "protect the canal." The speed with which Israel accomplished her objectives surprised even her allies. It also proved a point. Egypt, even though backed and heavily armed by the Soviet Union, was no match for the young Israeli Defense Force. And while, in the peculiar way Arabs tend to interpret events, Nasser in defeat was viewed as a hero, Israel bought a few years of relative calm on her borders.

This lull would provide Zvi with his first real opportunity to concentrate on the business of settling into a state of permanency in his chosen land.

Over the next few years, the Lord would do marvelous things in mending the holes shot through Zvi's life by the Holocaust. Home base was shifted from the transit camp in Talpiyot to private quarters. His second move after he left the camp had him in a much better location in Jerusalem. Best of all, it put him in close proximity to Esther, the young Jewish immigrant from Iran who was destined to become his bride.

One by one, the children began to shape the family circle. Ruth was first in 1960. Mendel joined her in 1962. Yona was next in 1964. And just as the Six-Day War was about to break out in 1967, Eli came upon the scene. With his birth, Zvi and Esther's family was complete. The Lord, in His grace and goodness, has restored to Zvi what Hitler had cruelly taken. Three brothers and a sister were swept away with his parents. Three sons and a daughter now entered his life as if sent to fill the place made empty during the war in Europe.

As the children grew in stature, Zvi and Esther were rapidly growing in grace and knowledge of the Lord. The love for the Bible which Zvi had experienced upon receiving his first New Testament became a pleasurable lifestyle. He was, without question, a man of the Book. As head of the house, he was always ready to share the knotty questions about Scripture and *living the life* that came up with Esther or one of the children. They were active in the church. When the doors were opened, the Weicherts were there. And they were available for whatever service their hands could find to render for the glory of God. This was very literally the case as they took responsibility for the physical needs of the building. Zvi was right for the job. As a construction worker, he was a man who knew how to work with his hands and was always willing to pitch in. He was particularly pleased when he could use his hands in the service of the Lord.

Esther enjoyed it too. She was a young woman who had an aversion to anything even remotely akin to dirt. And helping keep things squeaky clean was a challenge she was not capable of resisting.

An objective observer could see that the Lord was preparing these two for some very special service. They were vessels He planned to use. Among the first challenges they faced was living among those who took militant exception to what they believed and stood for as followers of Jesus, the Messiah.

Little Ruthi would be the first of the children to feel the lash of ultra-Orthodox bigotry.

27

CHAPTER THREE

BEAT HER!

S he cried all the way home. "Mama! Mama! They hit me! They hurt me!" Esther understood very well what had happened, and why. It would take some time for Ruthi to begin to understand their problem.

The family had moved into a western suburb of Jerusalem which had a large concentration of ultra-Orthodox people. Their black-garbed brethren looked askance at the neighbors who bore none of the distinguishing marks of what they believed to be proper Judaism. Zvi's daughter had felt the sting of hands against her flesh one Shabbat when her Orthodox playmates heard sounds of a radio news report filtering from the Weichert home — a grave breech of Sabbath tranquility. For the most part, though, they were tolerated as *Goya* would be, and their children romped about the neighborhood playing their games.

Ruthi's rude awakening came at the hands of a loved and trusted grandfather figure, an old man named Rabbinowitz. The strictly observant elder was a great favorite of neighborhood children. He was fond of distributing candies and gentle pats on their heads. Old Rabbinowitz was a great storyteller, and this was what she liked best of all. The children would sit clustered around him for long periods, enthralled by his animated gestures and intriguing tales.

One pleasant afternoon, the old man was standing on his stairs passing out candies to an excited swarm of boys and girls. When laughing Ruthi reached up to her friend for her piece, she was rudely refused. "You — children — beat her," he ordered. The others, eager to please their benefactor, sent the startled girl running toward home with a barrage of slaps and catcalls.

Rabbinowitz had discovered that the cute little Weichert girl was not just another nonreligious Jew. She was the daughter of believers in Jesus.

29

His command to the children was a crude way of sending his message of disapproval to Zvi and Esther. It was the exhibition of an old animosity — a demonstration illustrating that, in Israel, some things haven't changed in two thousand years. As long as Zvi was just another nonpracticing Jew, perhaps even an atheist, he was tolerated. But as a Jew who believed in "that Jew, Jesus," his presence was unacceptable.

Mendel would bear the same identifying mark during their days in Ir Ganim. One boy, in particular, took great delight in calling out at every opportunity: "Hey, look at him — Mendel the Christian!" To Jews steeped in rabbinic Judaism, calling someone a Christian is worse than cursing him. To a child anxious to be accepted as a boy among boys, it was a heavy indignity to bear.

To a large extent, it was the ultra-Orthodox element in Israel that exacted a heavy toll on Zvi's family and other believers. Their lack of compassion for unobservant fellow Jews was as obvious as their black garments. Their conduct is one of the great incongruities of the modern state of Israel. Jewish people, scorned — hated and assailed among inhospitable Gentiles for centuries simply because of who they were — are now being scorned, hated and assailed by their own Jewish brothers, simply because they will not conform to sectarian strictures. That sad fact has torn the nation since her rebirth, and the scars of resentment run deep.

A secretary to a former prime minister, a nonreligious Jewess, harbors caustic memories of their unapologetic hypocrisy. "It was during the siege of Jerusalem in 1948. We, in the city, were on the verge of starvation. Our survival was very much an open question in those days. The Arabs had control of the Tel Aviv-Jerusalem road and supplying the city with food became virtually impossible.

"Then our boys managed to scrape a road, beyond the reach of Arab guns, through the hills to the city. They were heroes who had risked their lives to save us — some died in the effort. But when they came into the city with food, those idiots stoned the trucks carrying the food to save Jerusalem because it happened to be Shabbat.

"I can never forget how I felt the next day, when I saw those same men pushing people aside to get their hands on the food that was carried by the trucks they had stoned the day before."

She would gladly have returned the missiles to the black-clad oppressors with appropriate velocity.

The woman and many of her fellow Israelis shared understandable resentment toward the ultra-Orthodox. They have been the single most disruptive influence in the Jewish community.

Branches of the Hasidim manifest a variety of extremes. Some are active participants in the affairs of the Jewish state, while others refuse to recognize the legitimacy of Zionist Israel altogether. Most Hasidics wear the special garb familiar to travelers in the Holy Land. Their long black coats *(kapotes)* and black or fur hats *(spodiks)* set them apart in a manner reminiscent of the ostentatious Pharisees of Jesus' day. Most of them wear beards and carefully nurtured earlocks *(pe'ot)*.

The term *Hasidim* was used in rabbinic literature to designate those who maintained a higher standard in observing the religious and moral commandments. Hasidim from its inception promoted joy, dance and song as expressions of piety and prime factors in living the good Jewish life. Modern remnants of these "men of piety and good deeds" often bear little evidence of being worthy of the ideal.

One of the qualifying elements in the Hasidic system is a fanatical loyalty to charismatic personalities who provide leadership for the movement. These Rebbes, called *zaddiks*, provide the spiritual illumination for the individual Hasid and the Hasidic community from "his own all-pervasive radiance, attained through his mystic union with God." The *zaddik* is viewed as a wonder healer and miracle worker. In the eyes of his followers, he is a combination of confessor, moral instructor and practical adviser. He is also their theoretical teacher and exegetical preacher.

"In Hasidim the *zaddik* is conceived of as the ladder between heaven and earth, his mystic contemplation linking him with the Divinity, and his concern for the people and loving leadership tying him to earth. Hence his absolute authority, as well as the belief of most Hasidic dynasties that the *zaddik* must dwell in visible affluence" (*Encyclopedia Judaica*).

Thus, this segment of ultra-Orthodox Jewry follows a small group of powerful leaders, each with his own contingent of unquestioning followers to whom he is the authoritative representative of God and His exclusive interpreter. In reality, these Rebbes are revered as mini-messiahs — messiahs who are militantly at odds with *the* Messiah, Jesus.

For his part, Zvi opted for a course of action much different from that of the prime minister's secretary. He chose a *bread for a stone* approach. "If these people are ever to come to the light," he reasoned, "it will be by dropping a seed at a time before them. Show them kindness, give them the Word of God. It is the only way."

His perception and patience would be tested with neighbors like Ruthi's tormentors. The severest tests, however, were to come in the yeshivahs (Talmudic schools) — the hallowed ground of extreme ultra-Orthodoxy in Mea Shearim.

31

The shabby quarter's entrance is marked by a warning: "Jewish daughter — The Torah obligates you to dress with modesty. We do not tolerate people passing through our streets immodestly dressed." The 'Jewish daughters' who inhabit the area fit the prescription perfectly. Long, plain dresses hang loosely over thick-stockinged legs and heavy, styleless shoes. Kerchiefed heads bob behind ever present baby carriages, as the wives of the pious go about their shopping and errands.

Streets are littered with trash, and squalid buildings appear as prime candidates to be condemned. It's obvious that the dwellers of Mea Shearim have their minds on something beside local beautification programs. Just where their minds are is found inside the yeshivahs themselves.

Approaches up staircases into the *Schul* (school) often appear little better cared for than the rest of Mea Shearim. Narrow passages open into austere rooms occupied by the boys who attend daily classes. They move about in unregimented groups wearing white shirts, buttoned to the top, black pants, with tassels from *tallit* (prayer shawls) worn under the shirts flapping about their hips. Long curled earlocks swing under *yarmulke* (skullcaps) covering shaved heads.

The inner sanctum, where adult males spend innumerable hours hunched over their cherished commentary books, is another world altogether. Ornately decorated walls rise toward stately ceilings. One yeshivah has magnificent paintings of the symbols of Israel's twelve tribes gracing the ceiling. A raised, banistered platform stands in the center of the room with candelabra placed at intervals about the table from which the Torah is read. Exquisitely carved woodwork with elaborate niches supported by large marble pillars frames the ark which contains the Torah scrolls. Above the veiled chamber where the scrolls rest is a large gold crown placed directly above replicas of Moses' tables of stone inscribed with the Ten Commandments. The veil itself is royal blue with rich gold fringe and golden Magen David sown into the corners. Another crown and richly embellished Torah scrolls are embroidered into the fabric.

From this impressive riser, their messiah-figure Rebbe addresses his ecstatic perpetual students who jam the room on festive occasions.

Zvi was a familiar face as he moved through the streets and into the yeshivahs of Mea Shearim. His boldness seemed rather like that of a man walking unarmed into the proverbial lion's den — a situation inadvisable for most. But Zvi came uniquely equipped, properly burdened and unimpeded by a lack of courage. Watching him witness to the black-garbed denizens of the ultra-Orthodox quarter could evoke but one logical conclusion: only God could prepare a man to do this.

Zvi's foremost credential was his fluency in Yiddish, the favored tongue of the Hasidim. Hebrew is regarded as the holy language and is reserved for reading the Torah. His approach was always direct, but kind and tactful. And somehow, one had the inescapable feeling that the Holy Spirit was at work in keeping the peace and opening opportunities for him to share the Lord.

There were a few times when open hostility made a quick exit an advisable option, and dodging saliva missiles enlivened the exchanges. Once Zvi found himself circling to the rear of a building to elude irate pursuers who took exception to his words. But this was the rare exception, not the rule.

One such excursion found him bounding up the steps, armed only with his Bible, to a yeshivah with a sign out front proclaiming the Solomonic desire for "Wisdom, Understanding, Knowledge." It was afternoon, and the attitude was much more relaxed than in the morning when intensive study was going on.

Wisdom called for some casual conversation which would break the ice and perhaps open the way to a witness for Christ. Within a short time, Zvi was probing with questions about just what their revered Rebbe taught on certain subjects. "And what do you believe about Zechariah 9:9: 'Rejoice greatly, O daughter of Zion; shout, O daughter of Jerusalem; behold, thy King cometh unto thee; he is just, and having salvation; lowly, and riding upon an ass, and upon a colt, the foal of an ass'?"

"This is without explanation," a rabbi responded, as others began to join the proceedings.

"Well then," Zvi continued, "maybe you can explain a passage that has been in my mind for some time. It is Isaiah 53."

"That passage is not familiar to me," the rabbi answered.

"Perhaps I could read it for you and refresh your memory."

"If you know Hebrew, go ahead, read it."

Zvi read the verses slowly and carefully.

When he finished reading, he looked intently into the face of the man standing before him. "Could you please explain the sixth verse: 'All we like sheep have gone astray; we have turned every one to his own way, and the LORD hath laid on him the iniquity of us all.' "

The man stroked his beard thoughtfully before he gave his reply. "The answer to your question will come when the Messiah will come."

"But this is very strange to me," Zvi countered. "You have studied here since you were three years old and don't have an answer to this question."

"Some things are hard to understand."

"If you would like, I will give you an explanation," Zvi said with a boldness that even startled him.

"Who was He? I am sure you know but will not say. It must be speaking of Jesus, who was crucified."

Tension built with his statement. "You have come to the wrong place with talk like this," a man in the circle fumed.

"No, I have come to the right place and asked you questions you should be asking yourselves.

"You know as well as I that our whole system for forgiveness of sin is built on the offering of proper sacrifices. Why, then, was our Temple destroyed and the offering of all sacrifices stopped — but only after the crucifixion took place?"

"We are Jews here," called out another angry voice. "Do you want to make us Christians?"

"No. I want to make you good Jews."

"But you are not a Jew, you are a Christian."

"I am as much a Jew as you are. But I am one who believes in Jesus. And why? Because I believe in the Bible. We can be Jews and believe the whole Word of God.

"Answer for yourselves. If I don't tell you what the Bible says, do what you will to me. But you must ask yourselves, 'What does this mean? What does Isaiah 9:6 mean when it says, "For unto us a child is born, unto us a son is given, and the government shall be upon his shoulder; and his name shall be called Wonderful, Counselor, The Mighty God, The Everlasting Father, The Prince of Peace"?' Yes, and many other Scriptures you ignore while reading the rabbi's fables."

As the conversation grew more intense, Zvi felt a quickening kinship to the Apostle Paul in his volatile exchanges with the forebears of his audience.

Upon leaving the yeshivah, He was grateful for God's protection. His opponents had uncharacteristically invited him to sit with them for coffee before his departure. This and other subtle indicators led him to believe that some light had penetrated the spiritually murky atmosphere of that place. The Lord's Word had given them food for thought, and perhaps some pointed inquiries for their Rebbe.

In any case, it had been seed sown. He would pray that some fell on good ground.

1967 — 1973

CHAPTER FOUR

SIX DAYS IN JUNE

F or the Western world, World War I (1914-1918) was "the war to end all wars." History would quickly dispel such naive wishful thinking. Zvi and much of Israel flirted with the same delusion about the Six-Day War (June 5-10, 1967). It would, indeed, prove to be the high-water mark in the short history of the modern state of Israel. Jewish emotions would spiral to dizzying heights — Abraham's sons and daughters had seen nothing equivalent to it for millennia. The euphoria would last only a few years, but this war gave the nation her most spectacular singular achievement: the reunification of Jerusalem.

From beginning to end, this war was different. To begin with, it was preemptive. That is, Israel started it in order to use the element of surprise against enemies who were poised to attack her once again. Shortly after 7:00 a.m. on June 5th, 183 Israeli aircraft swarmed over 11 Egyptian air bases making a shambles of Gamal Abdel Nasser's air force. The handwriting was on the wall for the Arabs from the second the first bomb struck.

An overwhelming sense of history in the making accompanied the opening sortie. As Israeli planes began their initial bombing runs, a coded message was received: " 'Nahshonim, action. Good luck.' Nahshon, leader of the tribe of Judah during the Exodus, is traditionally believed to have been the first to enter the waters of the Red Sea as they parted, setting the example to the rest of the Children of Israel, who promptly followed" (Moshe Dayan).

Two days later, Nahshon's modern colleagues in courage would be standing atop Abraham's Moriah sending out the heart-stopping message: "The Temple Mount is ours!"

Historians, national leaders and men of war would be captivated by Israel's military victory for decades to come. For the women and children who stayed behind, it was quite another story.

37

For them, the big difference was that they were in the middle of the war zone. Jerusalem was a battlefield. The last engagement of consequence with the Arabs had been the Sinai campaign in 1956. It had lasted only 100 hours and was fought far from Israel's centers of population. So in Jerusalem and other towns and cities, it was business as usual. This luxury was not theirs in June, 1967.

King Hussein of Jordan had received some bad advice from his Egyptian allies. "We were," he would later lament, "the recipients of false information about what had happened in Egypt...." His was one of the classic understatements of the war. Nasser and his generals told the king that their forces were winning sweeping victories and were crushing Israeli bases. Based on this information, Hussein decided to honor his pact with Egypt and join the effort to "drive Israel into the sea" — it was the biggest mistake of his political life.

About mid-morning on June 5th, Jordanian forces began heavy artillery shelling of Israeli villages and towns, including the outskirts of Tel Aviv. They also bombed a number of inhabited areas from the air. The major brunt of the shelling was felt in Jerusalem; and at 11 a.m., Jordanian ground forces began their attack in Jerusalem.

Five-year-old Mendel, Zvi's oldest boy, was playing with a friend in the yard when Hussein's gunners opened fire. "We were playing in the garden, near the fence [it marked the border between Jewish and Arab territory] when the sirens went off. It was a new sound to us, so we didn't know exactly what we were supposed to do.

"There was a valley beyond the fence, and we couldn't see into it. Our imagination had created visions of a huge elephant living over in the valley. I called to my friend, 'Hey, maybe the siren means the elephant is coming! Let's go to the fence and see.' So there we were, sitting by the fence, looking toward the valley on the Arab side."

Their childish fantasy was shattered when he looked up to see his mother running toward them carrying newborn Eli wrapped in a blue hospital blanket. Esther wore a stricken look on her face as she began to scream, "Mendel! Mendel! Come! Hurry! We must get into the shelter."

When the boys saw other neighbors running toward the shelter too, they knew the game was over. The scene had turned ugly; it was time for them to run for their lives.

The shelter was small and overcrowded. Light was filtering through the windows in strange crisscrossed patterns fashioned by the masking tape stuck to the windows to discourage flying glass fragments. It gave an eerie look to the place as it fell on fear-twisted faces and merged with the muffled sounds and vibrations from artillery fire. Those noises intruding into their small haven were not reassuring. The roar from aircraft swooping overhead, the bombs, and the pop-pop-pop of small arms fire made little hearts race against lungs already straining for breath. It was all much too close for comfort.

After a while, Mendel left the huddled family groups and made his way toward the door of the shelter. Trembling, he began to pray for abba to appear at the door of the shelter and tell him that everything was OK. Perhaps, he thought, God would think him more earnest if he imitated the Hasidic Jews he had watched praying from time to time. Methodically, he began rocking back and forth as if to engage the entire body in the act of prayer and prove to God just how serious he was. If only father would come, as he always did, his bad dream would be over. They could all go home again.

Mendel's earnestness and fears were not misplaced. Even as a five-year-old child, he knew the facts of life for Israel in her wars for survival.

"I would sit listening to the guns," he would later remember, "with one thing in my mind: If we lose, I won't be alive for ten minutes."

Women and children are not the only victims of anguish when men go off to fight their nation's battles. Men of war experience troubles of their own.

Zvi had a very real problem when the soldiers came bearing the red notice card ordering him to report for duty. The Six-Day War had not actually begun, but because of the nature of his responsibilities, Zvi was required to report early. (For Zvi, the Six-Day War meant eighty days of service.)

Almost from the time he had entered the Israeli Defense Force in 1948, Zvi practiced the ticklish business of planting or removing various types of mines. It was the "every time a perfect job" section of the service. His commander's first words were as fresh to his mind, after nearly twenty years, as they were the day he first heard them.

"You are going into an interesting business, one you will have just cause to be proud in doing well. This is the only department in the army of Israel where you must do a perfect job every time. When you are working with the mines, you only get one mistake. You will not get the chance to make the same error twice."

Before he had family responsibilities, he didn't think a great deal about himself or his situation at any given time. But now it was different, he had three kids at home and no mother there to look after them. That thought gnawed at his insides relentlessly as the beginning of the war approached. He was a man distracted, doing a job that did not make allowances for distractions.

When he was called to duty, Esther was in the hospital delivering Eli. She experienced complications during the birth which necessitated an extended stay.

"You see my problem," Zvi explained to his commanding officer, "I have no one to take care of my children. If I could just have a little time to call someone in."

"I can appreciate your situation," he was told, "but there is really no alternative. You must go, and you must go immediately. Don't worry, we have capable volunteers available. I'll have someone sent right over."

The officer was true to his word. Almost within minutes, it seemed, the temporary mother was at the door.

"Good evening," she said with a smile, "I'm Rebecca. I'm here to take care of the children."

Zvi took a look at Rebecca the baby-sitter. "Oi," he murmured to himself, "this one needs a sitter herself."

He had a question for the young lady who was about to play mother to his children: "How old are you, child?"

"Fourteen," was her cheerful reply.

"Do you know about caring for children?"

"Oh yes, I do it all the time."

He wasn't convinced, but he had already taken more time than the army wanted to allow him. "Here," I'm giving you all the money I have. It should be enough to last until I return."

So Zvi was off to help get the nation ready for war. Rebecca would tend the home fires for the three Weichert wards he was forced to leave behind.

Under the circumstances, one can understand why Zvi's mind kept leaping from the minefields to the hospital to the house and back again. These were tough days for abba.

As soon as his unit returned to the Jerusalem sector, Zvi requested permission to make a quick visit to his home in Ir Ganim.

"I'll do better than give you permission for the visit," the officer who knew about his predicament said, "I'll arrange for a car to take you there."

He was dismayed when he entered the house. It looked as though a volcano had erupted in the middle of the living room. A grimy-faced Ruthi ran to him with outstretched arms. "Oh, abba, we love Rebecca," she chirped.

"And just why do you love Rebecca?" he asked, trying hard to cover his astonishment.

"Because she gives us candy and ice cream."

Mendel, too, thought Rebecca had taken them to paradise. "In the morning, candy. At noon, ice cream. In the evening, maybe some of each."

Where, they wondered, had their mother been when such wonderful lessons in how to feed children were being taught? She certainly hadn't paid as much attention as had their sitter friend, Rebecca.

The only break in the sweets routine came when Uncle Nathan showed up at the door with two cartons of eggs. Nathan was a family favorite from the church who was challenging sniper fire to deliver food during the crisis. His eggs seemed rather common fare compared to Rebecca's exotic offerings.

Not only had the sitter exhausted the funds Zvi had provided, but her somewhat extravagant food service had put him in debt at the neighborhood market. It would take awhile to dig himself out.

Friends from the church came to the rescue. And Zvi was not sorry to send Rebecca back to her home. He was in a much better frame of mind when he went back to the grim business of war. His children, left in orderly surroundings, were scrubbed, well fed and cared for by people who adhered to Esther's family menu plan.

When the episode was all over and things had settled down, Zvi had a good, long laugh. First, he laughed about Rebecca. Poor child, she would have to do a lot of polishing on her prowess as a homemaker before she would be ready for matrimony. Zvi could just see her giving a chocolate party every day for a husband and children without a tooth in their collective heads because of her skills with the sweets.

His heartiest laugh, however, was reserved for himself, because he was afflicted by a common human frailty. In close proximity to someone else's failure, it is easy to forget your own failures, and he had a big one to remember when it came to cooking.

After the fighting ended in 1949, he was assigned a bed in the caboose-like barracks at the transit camp in Talpiyot. His bunk mates were immigrants from Morocco who, like himself, had fought with the army. After they got around the language barrier and adjusted to one another's personal habits, they became good friends who shared and shared alike.

The Moroccans took turns cooking, while Zvi did his part by paying a share of the cost of their food. One day, they had business that would keep them away for most of the afternoon. "Zvi," they said, "it's about time you began taking your turn at the stove. This is a good day for you to begin. Today you will be responsible for our supper."

While Zvi had had a great deal of experience as a scrounger, he had never done any serious cooking to speak of.

"I can't guarantee the result," he called after them. "I've never done much cooking."

41

"It's easy," they shot back. "You can do it."

Of course he was sure he could do it. He could do just about anything he set his mind to.

The stove was one of those kerosene contraptions with two or three burners that billowed great clouds of black smoke if you turned it up too high or the wick was bad. Zvi fired it up and rummaged through their meager supply of pots to find one to his liking. He made his selection, dumped in healthy portions of rice and beans, then poured oil over the whole concoction.

He was quite pleased with himself. His no-frills meal was also no fuss, and he found himself with time on his hands as he waited for his culinary masterpiece to finish cooking.

"I may as well go to town for awhile," he told himself. "I'll be back in plenty of time to have things ready for the fellows."

So, off he went to enjoy a couple of leisurely hours amid friends on the streets of Jerusalem.

As he was returning, he could see a plume of black smoke rising in the air above the camp. "I knew it would happen someday," he said to a friend who was walking in the same direction. "Some of those old women at the camp are so feeble they can hardly get around, much less take care of themselves. I'm surprised one of them hasn't burned a barracks down before this."

Once Zvi got into the camp, he saw that the smoke was suspiciously close to his own barracks — or what had formerly been his own barracks. Wisps of smoke were about all that remained of the place he and the Moroccans had called home. Later, when he dug around in the rubble, he located the charred pot and remnants of the stove. Wouldn't you know — the rice and beans were ruined.

"Well, at least," he chuckled to himself, "Rebecca didn't burn the house down. Maybe, if I see her again, I'll tell her that story and give her some advice about cooking. On second thought, I'll have Esther give her a few pointers about kitchen conduct."

CHAPTER FIVE

MOVE, MOVE, MOVE!

F ighting in Jerusalem during the Six-Day War was to have a profound affect on Israel, Jewry, Arabs, the superpowers and the world at large. The religious impact alone was monumental. Within a few hours, messianic tides would begin to be evidenced which will one day be consummated at the great second advent of Jesus Christ. Whatever can or cannot be said about hard biblical confirmation of modern Israel's place in prophecy, all must agree that the reunification of Jerusalem demonstrated that something was going on among Jewish people which could not be humanly orchestrated.

The wider war not only changed the face of the geography of the Middle East, it altered fundamental facts of life for the region. With the cessation of hostilities, Israel was no longer as vulnerable to attack as she had been because of the way armistice lines were drawn in 1949. She now had ample warning time if intemperate enemies decided to start another war. Jordanian artillery was denied its Judean hills emplacements, and terrorists would find much more difficulty reaching Israeli population centers. In the north, the Syrians could no longer take potshots at Jewish kibbutzim.

Israel's political and diplomatic situation also changed dramatically. Before the war, it had little to bargain with. Afterward, it had territories to use as valuable bargaining chips with Arab states who were beginning to get the message: They were not going to bully Israel to the wall by weight of arms. It was the Arabs who were pleading with the United Nations and the superpowers to get Israel off their backs before IDF soldiers were taking in the sights in Damascus, Cairo or Amman.

Prophetic shadows were reflected in the fact that the superpowers were now clearly in the conflict. The United States and parts of Western Europe were aligned with Israel, while the Soviet Union was intruding on behalf of Arab client states.

But for Zvi and most of his Israeli brethren, Jerusalem was where the action would be centered.

Fierce fighting raged in Jerusalem and around the Old City all day and most of the night on June 6th. Zvi and his sapper comrades were hard pressed to open lanes through the minefields for men and tanks.

Teddy Kolleck, who later became Mayor of united Jerusalem, remembers their heroism. In describing fighting around the Rockefeller Museum, he said: "The tanks were there only because while fighting was going on in the Police School, paratroop sappers were clearing a path through the minefield alongside the school compound. It took them several pre-dawn hours, for they were under continuous and accurate shellfire, mostly from 81-mm guns, and mine clearing had to be done by hand between salvos. They would rush out from cover during the brief lulls, clear a few mines, and then race back as the rounds came over."

Caution was thrown to the winds in those desperate and decisive hours when getting lethal mines out of the way of advancing troops was more than a choice, it was indispensable if Jerusalem was to be taken.

Teddy Kolleck recalls that troops were "bent on speed, even at the cost of higher casualties. They had no flailer tanks to crash through the minefields — these were all in Sinai — so their sappers simply cleared the mines by hand with prod and knife. Operating in daylight and under fire from the enemy on high ground, they suffered forty casualties in less minutes from enemy fire and exploding mines."

This cut cross-grain to all Zvi's instruction and instincts in handling these deadly devices. He had seen the high cost of hurry exacted too many times over his years of service to his country, and he carried many reminders in his mental notebook.

Working deliberately was an absolute necessity in the mine planting/removal business. "If I work quick, I will go quick," he kept telling himself. Since he had come to know the Lord, he had learned a settled sense of patience as well. Second Timothy 2:24 taught him, "the servant of the Lord must...be...patient." No need to hurry. One step at a time; one day at a time. God is in control.

Some others had not yet come to his settled lifestyle in the Lord, however, and they didn't quite understand Zvi's operational procedures.

One day, while he and the men he commanded — Zvi was a sergeant at the time — were clearing an area where the Arabs had planted mines, a young officer gave him a dressing down.

"You are working like a grandfather," chided the youngster. "If you don't get a move on, you will never finish this job."

"The Arabs," Zvi explained, "have planted mines like potatoes in this place, there is no pattern to them, and we don't know where they are. We must move slowly or we will lose men."

The officer, long on schooling and short on experience, didn't want to hear that kind of talk.

"You get out of here. I will do your work and show the men how it's done."

Zvi didn't want to leave the scene, but he had no choice. An officer had issued an order. He had no alternative but to obey. He knew all too well the danger his hot-headed superior was walking into. The Arabs did not follow the rules of war prescribed for civilized nations by the Geneva Convention. Their mines were planted indiscriminately with no discernable patterns or retrieval maps. They had also learned the nasty trick from the Germans of planting sandwich mines — one on top of the other. So when one was being pulled up, it would detonate the one beneath it.

Within a matter of minutes, Zvi and his comrades were straightened up by the dull "wump" of an exploding anti-personnel mine. The young officer, minus a foot and part of a hand, was unconscious on the ground. The war was over for him.

"It is so sad," Zvi told his buddies, "the same thing could have happened to any one of us. But as long as we keep moving with the caution of grandfathers, we have a chance of seeing our families again."

But this was a time when there was no time, so he worked feverishly with a little phrase repeatedly running through his mind: "Trust in the Lord; what will be, will be."

With Zvi and the sappers opening the way, the Old City was encircled by Jewish forces, and the dawn of June 7th found young Israelis poised to attack the Mount of Olives and make their heart-stopping charge on the walls of the Old City.

The sense of history and destiny was as brightly before them that morning as the brilliant Jerusalem sun cutting through the choking smoke of battle. Even the participants seemed to have been ordered to the place in a precise display of planning from an unseen hand.

General Moshe Dayan, fabled one-eyed warrior and recently appointed Minister of Defense, passed the High Command's attack order to IDF Central Forces Commander, Major General Uzi Narkiss. Narkiss was the Palmach Brigade commander who in 1948 briefly penetrated the Old City but was denied the prize by too much enemy pressure and too little time before the cease-fire.

45

Narkiss, in turn, issued the order to Colonel Mordechai "Motta" Gur. For years, the young soldier had sketched plans in his mind and rehearsed his brigade for this moment, should the opportunity ever come. Colonel Gur was one of Jerusalem's native sons, yet because of nineteen years of Jordanian refusal to open the Old City to Jews, he had been denied access to his birthright — that injustice would be corrected shortly.

Also on hand was Chief Chaplain of the Forces, Major General Rabbi Shlomo Goren. His presence completed the symbolic encapsulation of Israel's strength, national heart's desire and transcending religious dream of dreams — to possess *their* Holy City: Jerusalem.

Indeed, it would take a rabbi to say it best for all of Jewry: "To us the world is like an eye. The white is everything else. The iris is Israel, Land of the Jews. And the pupil, it is, of course, the Holy City, Jerusalem. But the gleam in the center of the pupil — that gleam is Moriah, the Temple Mount."

Young Motta Gur was so taken with the historical moment and a desire to pay it due respect that he commanded his half-track driver, a bearded farmer from Galilee, to stop in mid-charge. They had raced down the southern slope of the Mount of Olives on a road that took them out of sight of the city. "Turn around," he shouted to his somewhat confused subordinate. "Drive up to the overlook in front of the Intercontinental Hotel. I want to give the command for the conquest of the Old City from an appropriate place."

Ignoring strict regulations against giving unit designations on the radio, he began. "Paratroop Brigade 55. We stand on the heights of the Old City. In a little while we will enter it — the ancient city of Jerusalem which for generations we have dreamed of and strived for. Our brigade has been given the privilege of being the first to enter.

"Move, move, move. Move to the gate!"

Their fervent response to his command will forever shine from the pages of Jewish history.

Soon members of the 55th were assembled before the Wailing Wall, and Gur was sending out his historic message telling the world that the Old City was safely in Jewish hands.

When the Chief Rabbi arrived, the shofar sounded before the stone wall in an act which heralded the reunification of the two Jerusalems, old and new. It also symbolically echoed throughout the far-flung world of Jewry inviting Jacob's sons and daughters to come back home. Ecstatic paratroopers hoisted Rabbi Goren to their shoulders, and he enjoyed an impromptu ceremonial ride, waving the shofar and Torah scroll wildly above his head.

To complete the fact of an Israeli presence on the Temple Mount, Gur's men hoisted the Israeli flag above the Islamic shrine, the Dome of the Rock. Their revelry over such an emblematic sight was, however, short-lived. When General Dayan came to the Wall with fellow Generals Narkiss and Rabin, he spotted the flag and ordered it removed.

Great words and symbols from that day would endure in the minds of participants and observers: the Torah cradled in a craggy niche in the giant stones — battle-blackened faces, streaked with tears, looking up at the wall with unbridled awe — a bespectacled boy-soldier, helmet in hand, yarmulke on his head and a shell-studded bandolier around his shoulders like a prayer shawl, leaning his forehead against a war-dirtied fist pressed hard to the stones.

"This is the greatest day of my life," said one of the state's most illustrious architects, David Ben-Gurion.

General Narkiss was speechless. "It was as though I was in another world — in a cloud of happiness....I felt a part of the whole Jewish people, who for two thousand years had longed for this."

But Moshe Dayan made the most compelling declaration of intent: "We have returned to our holiest of holy places.... We earnestly stretch our hands to our Arab brethren in peace, but we have returned to Jerusalem never to part from her again."

An appropriate tribute to the epochal events of the day had been presented only a few weeks before the fighting broke out. Naomi Shermer's hauntingly beautiful song, "Jerusalem of Gold," had been introduced to the nation at the Independence Day celebration held on May 15, 1967. Her stirring lyrics caught the mood and voiced universal Jewish commitment: "If I forget thee, O Jerusalem, may my right hand its cunning lose."

A bone-weary Zvi witnessed his countrymen's euphoria. He, too, had gold on his mind.

CHAPTER SIX

THE GOLDEN CALF

I n the final phases of the attacks prior to Israel's penetration of the Old City, Zvi was busy clearing mines with knife and probe near the Rockefeller Museum not far from Herod's Gate. His feet and legs were badly swollen from what seemed interminable hours of duty and the many changes of position made at full footspeed. He had been clearing entryways for tanks under withering fire, which often had them scampering for cover.

By the time the 55th Brigade was preparing to launch its conclusive assault, Zvi's unit had been moved to a position near the Dung Gate. Gur's initial plan to enter through Herod's Gate had been scrapped in favor of an assault through the Lion's Gate (St. Stephen's) on the eastern side. So, while members of Gur's brigade were making their entry, Zvi's group was preparing to enter from the south. Moshe Dayan described activities there:

"As they were entering the Old City from the east, Eliezer Amitai's Jerusalem Brigade was about to enter from the south, through the Dung Gate. His troops did so half an hour later, having captured several Arab positions and cleared the minefields between Mount Zion and the Church of Peter in Gallincantu. It was soon after this that I entered liberated Jerusalem and visited the Western Wall."

Like his fellow Jews who were privileged to be at the scene during these momentous moments, Zvi was grateful that Jerusalem was no longer a divided city. David's words were in his mind as he watched the near dilerium gripping the soldiers at the Wall. "I was glad when they said unto me, Let us go into the house of the LORD. Our feet shall stand within thy gates, O Jerusalem. Jerusalem is builded as a city that is compact together...Pray for the peace of Jerusalem; they shall prosper who love thee. Peace be within thy walls, and prosperity within thy palaces" (Ps. 122:1-3, 6-7).

How deeply he longed for peace within her walls, for an end to killing and a good life for his family in the City of Peace. He felt all of this. But, strangely, Zvi did not feel the fervent exhileration he saw in his fellow victors. He watched and listened as Rabbi Goren sounded his ram's horn, and Narkiss led the troops in Israel's national hymn, Hatikvah. "But why do we conduct ourselves so before a wall of stones?" he wondered.

"We have our city. Good. This is a wonderful day in the history of Israel. But this is not a holy place. It is a wall built around our ancient Temple by an enemy, Herod. There is nothing sacred here."

Indeed, the Arabs had done their best to desecrate the spot so revered by his Jewish brethren. They had given literal meaning to the gate named Dung. It was piled high in the narrow street, so near the Arab houses that Zvi wondered how anyone could stand to live with the flies and stench. To the Arabs, however, dung piled before Jewry's great shrine was a symbol of superiority. So was kicking over Jewish grave markers to use for stepping stones, and demolishing synagogues and buildings in the captured Jewish Quarter. It was all a matter of symbolism. Venerated placed and objects were knocked down by one belligerent, only to be raised again when their adversary prevailed and drove them from the hallowed ground.

Oh, Zvi understood symbolism very well. There is hardly a Jew alive on the earth who comes up short in that department. And he wasn't really objecting to national monuments. He was saddened for his people, who had returned after so long a time only to worship cold, lifeless stone. "This place," he thought dejectedly, "will become a new golden calf for Israel."

Moses' experience could be held before the nation as a solemn warning and an invitation. Before he could return from Sinai with his revelation of the Law from Jehovah's lips, they were reveling before a lifeless thing. The golden calf had taken the place of the living God. Moses' challenge rang in Zvi's mind: "Who is on the LORD's side? Let him come unto me" (Ex. 32:26).

Thoughts turned to the Temple built by King Solomon — Israel's first national house of worship — home for the Shekinah glory that flooded the Holy of Holies with the light of God's presence among His people. But Israel's disobedience and rebellion had so grieved the Lord that the Shekinah was replaced by Ichabod — "the glory has departed."

The Messiah came to a house of worship where its holiest chamber knew only darkness, and He drove out those who traded in Jehovah's courts to fill their pockets rather than empty hearts. "Make not my Father's house an house of merchandise" (Jn. 2:16), He told them. Zvi wondered what Jesus would say to them today.

"If they only realized that stones cannot save them," he cried out in his heart. "If only they would come to Him, instead of a wall, how wonderful this day would be."

Weeks later, while doing guard duty at night, he watched people coming to the Wall. The approaches through the streets were now cleaned of dung and debris. All through the night, they came. Through the Dung Gate, down the gentle descent, past the path leading up to the Temple platform, through the narrow street and on to the wall. Little groups of women and men came silently, as though they were entering a great cathedral. They positioned themselves there, dwarfed by the great stones, to weep and pray. Some rolled up pieces of paper containing their petitions and wedged them in the crevices between the stones.

Some of the women reminded him of Hannah, wife of Elkanah and mother of the Prophet Samuel, who came to the Temple greatly distressed to pray to the Lord and weep bitterly. She had been so overwhelmed in her agony and lamentation that the priest Eli thought she was drunk.

These women, many deeply lamenting their own darker days, perished dreams and shattered families, bent before the Wall like modern Hannahs.

While walking his post along the Wall one night, he stopped to speak to a woman who seemed particularly overwrought.

"I see you crying here before the stones. Why are you weeping?"

"I am a woman who has passed more trouble than you can ever know. I come here to find peace and an answer to my prayers."

"Dear lady, do you think your answer is here in these stones?"

"It is a sacred place," she replied.

"No, these stones are not God, who alone can answer your prayers. You must know the Lord. And when you know Him, you don't have to come through the streets of Jerusalem at night to pray before a wall. You can pray to Him there in your home, and He will give you your answer."

He would give that same bit of advice to many such troubled people over the nights and years to follow. Most would only turn again toward the lifeless stones to seek solace.

Twenty years later, Zvi and his son Eli stood not far from the spot where he talked with the woman. It was in the yeshiva under Wilson's arch where Orthodox Jewish men come to study and pray. There they encountered a man looking like someone who might have stepped out of the pages of history — perhaps one of David's "mighty men." He was big, young, most likely in his early twenties, with jet black hair and a full beard. A tefillah (box containing Scripture passages) was strapped to his head by leather strips just under his white yarmulke. His prayer shawl hung almost to his white running shoes, and a prayer book was open on the table beside him.

While Eli leaned against the railing around the deep shaft running down the wall, Zvi opened a conversation with the young Jew.

"Hello. How is everything going?"

"I'm doing OK, thank you."

"Do you live here in Jerusalem?"

"No, my home is in Tiberias. I came to Jerusalem to pray."

"And why did you come all the way to Jerusalem to make your prayers? Can't you pray in Tiberias?"

"Yes, of course, I can pray in Tiberias," the young man said, "but the Shekinah is not in Tiberias. It is here in the Old City. So I come here to pray near the Shekinah."

"Oh, I see," said Zvi, "but these are only stones. Do you mean to tell me you have come here to worship stones?"

"No, not stones. I have come here to be in the presence of God."

"Well, my friend, you have made a big mistake. The Shekinah was here many centuries ago, in the first Temple. But when our people sinned, the Shekinah was taken from the Temple. When this wall was built, the Shekinah was not in the Temple, and that building was destroyed. And in spite of all the praying that has been done here, see how our people have suffered.

"The trouble is that you are only praying from books, not from the heart. When you come to know the Lord, really know Him, you can pray from your heart. Why? Because the Shekinah will be living in your heart, that's why."

Zvi's listener was not pleased by what he was hearing, but he did not react the way the Orthodox sometimes do. He disagreed but remained respectful. Zvi and Eli had prayed before they left the house that their witness would not be human words only, but the Spirit's work in empowering His Word. Perhaps, like a small mustard seed, something was sown that would raise a question in his heart and one day the Shekinah would, indeed, reign within him.

Whatever the eventual outcome, their meeting shows that things haven't changed spiritually for Israel over the centuries.

The fact is, the Six-Day War raised more spiritual problems than it solved. While there were resounding surges of emotion unparalleled in modern times and tremendous historical implications, Israel's sweeping triumph took her even farther from an attitude of reliance on God.

Zvi met the prevailing mood head on when he was talking to fellow soldiers one night in the aftermath of the war. The conversation had settled on how strong and clever they had been to catch Egypt by surprise and then defeat three countries with such comparative ease.

"Did you ever think that this may not have been our own strength?" Zvi asked. "It might just be that God wanted to free us from so much pressure and to put Jerusalem back in our hands. We should give some thought to what the Prophet Zechariah said, 'Not by might, nor by power, but by my Spirit, saith the LORD of hosts' [Zech. 4:6].

"I think God wants to teach us that it is time to seek the Messiah. We can rejoice, as we are now, but it should be as Zechariah told the daughters of Zion to rejoice: 'Rejoice...thy King cometh unto thee; he is just, and having salvation' [Zech. 9:9]."

At that point, an officer broke in abruptly. "Now you are talking about Jesus. This is no place to bring up a subject of this kind. We'll have no more of such conversation."

The officer's opinion expressed the hostility and resentment often encountered by Zvi and fellow believers after the Six-Day War. At those times, Jesus' words to disciples of a much earlier day came to mind: "I send you forth as sheep in the midst of wolves" (Mt. 10:16). Israeli self-sufficiency was not, for the time being, open to question.

Israel, in the "We can do it" days following the Six-Day War, was, as a nation, a great deal like Zvi himself had been until he saw his need of the Lord. He survived the Holocaust, he fancied, because he was too smart for his pursuers and much too quick for them to corner. It was "Zvi, the master of his own destiny." Then he learned just how wrong he had been. Others, he confessed, were smarter and as quick. But they perished, while he did not. Why? He came to understand, in an intensely personal way, what Jeremiah meant when he said, "It is because of the LORD's mercies that we are not consumed" (Lam. 3:22). Then, and only then, was he ready to seek God's provision in the Messiah.

So, in the postwar days, Zvi and other believers met in their little assemblies to worship together, edify and encourage one another. They witnessed faithfully without much outward evidence of success. But they lived in the assurance that the Lord was doing His own work in a quiet and faithful way, and the day would come when many in the nation would feel acutely their need for help outside themselves.

CHAPTER SEVEN

BUT WHERE'S THE BABY?

An unpleasant part of army life in Israel is the necessity to occasionally enter civilian homes to search for arms. One day, following the Six-Day War, Zvi was on a detail working a short distance from Jerusalem on the road to Ramallah. The area was dotted with expensive villas occupied by affluent Arabs.

The usual ritual questions were asked of the owner of the house, a tall, solemn looking son of Ishmael.

"I must ask you if you have any weapons on the premises," Zvi began. "In the event you do, if you will turn them over to us, there will be no problems or further questions asked."

"No, I am a peaceful man, I do not keep guns in my home," the Arab replied.

"I'm afraid I must ask you to allow us to look through the house to be sure."

"If you insist. But I can assure you, you will find no weapons here."

Zvi entered and walked slowly through the house, poking into closets and would-be hiding places. When he returned to the spacious room where the man and his wife were seated, he noticed that the man of the house appeared extremely nervous. "Well," he told himself, "he looks like a man who has something to hide."

Over in one corner of the room, Zvi saw a baby carriage. It was completely covered with a light blanket. "Oh, I see you have a little one," he said, as he strode toward the carriage. When he glanced at the man, the Arab had a stricken look on his face. It appeared that the fellow, who had risen from his seat and was pursuing Zvi across the room, was about to pass out. Zvi was certain he was about to uncover implements intended to bring harm to Jews.

When he lifted the blanket, he was astonished to find it was filled to the top with gold, precious gems and U. S. dollars. Now Zvi's unwilling, scarlet-faced host did totter on the brink of falling to the floor. He propped himself against a piece of furniture and, with a resigned gesture, awaited the inevitable. The soldiers would promptly empty the buggy and make off with his treasure — or so he had been told.

This type of misinformation was disseminated liberally by Arab leaders in order to convince the population that, given the opportunity, the "Jewish devils" would loot their property to the last saleable item. That term "devil," Zvi would learn, was an appellation literally applied to the Jewish people by some Arabs.

When he was on duty in an isolated Arab village, he and his companions filled a large container with bread and began distributing it to Arab children. A swarm of eagerly receptive children kept making circles around the soldiers. When the soldiers asked the giggling kids what they were looking for, they ran a short distance, as if frightened that their maneuver had been detected. As soon as the soldiers were again occupied with passing out bread, small heads would be craning necks in an effort to see the soldiers' backsides.

One of the children's fathers, who had been observing from a respectful distance, walked over with a wide grin. "You know what they're looking for?" he said. "They want to see if Israeli soldiers really do have a devil's tail, as they have been told. Why don't you turn around and give them a good look."

It wasn't the only thing those youngsters had been told about Jews. In some Arab families, when children were reluctant to go to sleep, they were assailed with a recurring warning. "If you don't lie down and get to sleep right now, I will go get a Jew with horns and he will come and eat you alive!"

It was little wonder that the wealthy Arab feared the worst.

When Zvi turned from the contents, covered the carriage and was preparing to leave, the man's relief was tempered by a look of dismay.

"I was afraid you would take everything," he explained to the departing soldier.

Zvi, who after the Rebecca fiasco didn't have an agora in his pocket, replied with a hearty laugh, "No, yours is not the kind of treasure I'm looking for. The treasure that really concerns me is the treasure I have in Heaven."

Now the Arab was genuinely perplexed. "But we have heard that the Jews would take everything we have as spoils of war."

"Let me explain about Jews, and myself as a special Jew. No, Israeli soldiers will not take your personal belongings as spoils of war. And I will not take them for two reasons. The first you have heard already; the second is this: I was born a Jew, yes, but then I became a born-again Jew."

Perplexity turned to curiousity. "What do you mean by this phrase, 'born-again Jew'?"

"What I mean is, I am a Jew who believes in the Lord Jesus Christ as my Savior. So I have chosen to serve only the Lord God, not mammon.

"We have a song we sing in my church that expresses how it is. 'Nor silver nor gold has obtained my redemption. Nor riches of earth could have saved my poor soul. The blood of the cross is my only foundation. The death of the Savior now makes me whole.' "

You could have knocked the Arab over with a feather. "This is amazing," he exclaimed. "You see, I, myself, am not a Muslim. I am a Christian Arab."

So the Hebrew-Christian and the Arab-Christian found they were not enemies after all. They were, in fact, brothers in Christ!

Now the wealthy homeowner wanted to become a willing host. "Come back and sit with me. My wife will make coffee. You will be a welcomed guest in my home."

"That's very kind, but I'm afraid I must decline your offer," Zvi told him. "We are not allowed to eat or drink in homes where we are conducting searches. Maybe some other time."

Several months later, when he was walking through the Old City, Zvi was hailed by an insistent voice. "Hello! Hello! Hello!" It was the kind of urgent invitation tourists get accustomed to hearing from Arab merchants. This time, however, there was no intent to sell. When Zvi turned around, he found himself looking into the beaming face of the owner of the treasure-filled baby carriage. The man owned an antique shop in the Old City. It was a proper occasion for accepting hospitality, so Zvi and the merchant sat down together, drank coffee and talked of things common in Christ.

When Zvi found out, on a subsequent visit that his brother/friend had departed for Heaven, he was glad that God's providence had brought them together in the kind of relationship that money can't buy.

Zvi had had a thorough indoctrination in the "spoils of war" question long before he met the antique dealer.

Back in 1949, his unit had been transferred from the Jerusalem area to a camp near Tel Aviv. The cease-fire had been declared, and upon their departure from Jerusalem, some of the junior officers had gathered quite a number of "souvenirs" from the homes of Arabs who had fled the country. Arab leaders had urged them to do so, promising that when the war had been won, they could return to their homes and confiscate Jewish property as spoils of war. Now the shoe was on the other foot, and faced with the temptation, although it was forbidden, the officers indulged themselves with a few choice items to take home with them. When the truck containing the booty arrived at the new camp, it was quietly deposited in an out-of-the-way barracks for disposition at a later date.

Zvi and some of his friends from Europe were sitting together one day discussing the present state of their finances and prospects for future employment. "If we could only get our hands on some money," lamented one young man, "we could have the celebration we deserve after so much hard fighting."

"That may not be such a hard thing to do," said Zvi with a knowing look.

"What do you mean?" his companion asked. "I mean, I know how we can come by enough money to put on any kind of celebration we want."

"How?"

"Well, you know about the truckload of things those officers had brought over from Jerusalem and stored in the barracks. We have an ammunition truck to use. Tomorrow night, when we are on guard duty, we will load it on our truck, take it to Ramla, and sell it to the shopkeeper there who deals in such things."

"Count me out!" said the lad who made the inquiry. "I don't want to make that kind of trouble for myself."

"Now, wait a minute," responded another, who happened to be a lawyer. "Even the Talmud says it is not wrong to take from someone who has taken something illegally. They know as well as we do that they were not supposed to take those things. I agree with Zvi, we deserve a good time — and they could use the lesson. It will be good for them. Anyway, even if they catch us, where will they go to complain?"

The next night, the conspirators quietly rolled their vehicle alongside the barracks and began loading it up. The truck soon lumbered away toward Ramla with appointed representatives of their trading company ready to deal for the lot of it.

"You've got a lot of stuff here," observed the proprietor of the *no questions asked* establishment.

"I know," replied the bespectacled sales rep. "It ought to bring a pretty good price."

"Well, I don't know. There is so much of this kind of thing floating around these days, I really won't be able to get much for it."

So the dickering began. The boys didn't argue long. After all, they didn't have a great deal invested — just a little time and ingenuity.

When the man's offer came into range, the young entrepreneur yelled, "Sold!" and it was done. They slapped backs and congratulated themselves all the way back to camp.

The air had a festive feel as they carried in the meats and other embellishments. A brief meeting settled minor details. The guest list was the leading topic for discussion.

"Just to cover ourselves," suggested their resident intellectual, the lawyer, let's invite the officers to join us. It isn't necessary, really, but I think it's a nice touch, and a little more insurance won't hurt anything."

It turned out to be a memorable evening. Not one officer ventured to ask about the source of their capacity to put out such a spread. There were smiles all around when the evening ended and they took their satisfied stomachs to bed.

Smiles disappeared the next morning when the officers discovered what had happened. Zvi was among the first to be called on the carpet.

"You were in charge of the watch the night the barracks was emptied," a sullen officer charged.

"Yes, sir, I was," Zvi answered. "But may I say, I was not the only one on duty. Why am I called in as the chief suspect?"

Consequently, the whole detail was called in and questions began to fly. Their resident lawyer fielded the heavy queries.

"We frankly admit, sir, that we had some little part in the events in question. I suppose that the only recourse open now is to have the matter referred to higher authorities."

He was steering a straight line, and the officer knew exactly where the track would end. "You're dismissed for now. But I want you all to know you haven't heard the last of this."

His words had a foreboding ring to them, and they didn't have to wait long to get his drift — about two days for Zvi.

"Weichert, I want you to scrub the latrine today. I want it cleaned like it has never been cleaned before. When I inspect it, it had better be perfect, or you'll find out what trouble is all about."

"Yes, sir! It will be clean," promised his ramrod straight subordinate.

Zvi was seething inside. It was, he knew, pay day. His officer was after a generous pound of flesh. Zvi wasn't about to give him that satisfaction. These were the days before the Lord's grace had tempered his reactions, and a counter-injustice plan was almost instantly in place.

As a sapper, Zvi had access to the camp's explosives magazine. A little dynamite placed at strategic intervals would do a very nice job of cleaning the latrine "like it had never been cleaned before." It did. The explosion shook the camp and brought people running from all directions.

The officer was livid.

"But you said you wanted it cleaned as never before," Zvi reported. "As you ordered, it's clean."

"And I'm putting you up on charges," railed his superior.

"Do what you choose."

The senior officer who was selected to judge Zvi in the incident turned out to be a man he knew very well. He had served under him in Jerusalem. The officer also knew the reasons prompting the whole episode. The theft/sale/feast scenario was much too good a story to be kept under wraps — although the information was all quite unofficial.

"You have the right to stand before another officer if you wish," Zvi was told.

"No, sir. I will be pleased to have you as my judge."

The senior officer listened intently as particulars about the instant cleaning of the latrine were laid before him. When all the evidence was in, he sat back and announced his decision.

"First of all, let me say that I am well aware of what brought on this whole situation. And I want the entire matter dropped at once. The charges are dismissed. You are free to return to duty."

The junior officers were thus put on notice that there would be no more "spoils of war" activity or reprisals, and Zvi and his companions returned to less exotic pursuits of soldiering.

When the Six-Day War came to a close, Israel was not only in possession of the Old City of Jerusalem, she was also in control of the Gaza Strip, Golan Heights, West Bank of the Jordan and Sinai Desert. It would take some time for the Arabs to stop accusing one another of responsibility for the fiasco and get back to hounding Israel. Zvi would welcome the bit of breathing space this would give him and quickly got back to his first love, Esther and the kids. War had deprived him of more than a glimpse of his newest arrival, Eli. He was anxious to get home and see just what kind of stuff the boy was made of.

1973-1982

CHAPTER EIGHT

GROWING UP WITH LEGENDS

The Weichert children grew up surrounded by legends. They were really only men. But from the vantage point of the very small, who had to look up at everyone and virtually everything around them, these men seemed much larger than other mere mortals.

Father was the first and most ardently admired. To Ruthi, Mendel, Yona and Eli, he was like a proverbial man of steel. Muscles bulged from every member of his body. When they conspired to catch him by surprise, and piled on with war whoops and fierce fits of determination, he could raise them all to his shoulders and stride around the room as though he hadn't noticed they were pestering him. Each of the boys, in his turn, would attempt to dethrone him as the family arm wrestling champ. It was a waste of time — time that could better have been spent in some more fruitful enterprise.

Their walks through the streets of Jerusalem added to the aura. Strolls that would take ordinary people five or ten minutes would often stretch into an hour. Shouts of "Hey, Zvi!", "Hi Zvi!" or "Zvi! Wait a minute," were constantly impeding their progress. Old army buddies, people he had worked with and a seemingly endless procession of others all had something to say to Zvi and his kids. There's a saying that every Jew has a story. You didn't have to argue that theory with Zvi's children; they thought they had listened to them all — war stories, work stories, old country stories, etc., etc., etc.

They became accustomed to being thumped on the back by strong men as they passed along some commentary on father. "Ah, you are a lucky child to have such a one as this for a father — he is a good man. You want to grow up to be strong? Then be like your daddy."

This was all well and good and left an indelible constructive imprint on them all. But sometimes, for those intent on getting to the store for an ice cream cone, walking down King George or Ben Yehuda Streets could be an exercise in self-restraint. Also adding temper to the development of personal self-discipline was the stream of visitors pouring into their home. This was particularly bothersome to Mendel. No turf was guarded more tenaciously than Shabbat afternoons, when a boy could come home, eat a sumptuous meal, take the newspaper to his room, close the door, flop down on the bed and enjoy a serene siesta. Too often, or so it seemed to Mendel, he would open the door on a host of smiling faces offering "Shaloms" that did not add up to "peace" for his afternoon. Sometimes they would be local people, just in for the day. At other times, they came from far-off places and would be bedding down for a few days or weeks — perhaps in his bed!

Resentment of these unseemly intrusions began to fade as he grew to understand that these occasions were not designed to shatter Shabbat siestas but were an integral part of the ministry of hospitality so warmly extended to one and all by his parents.

Soon enough, he would learn that all of his legends, even abba, were only human beings after all — men with faults and frailties as real as anyone else's. But in the total process of growing up, these *legends* helped instill life's soundest lessons.

One frailty their father had was appearing to be a man who was perpetually broke. He never seemed to have two agora to rub together. Money for the pressing necessities that sustain life in small bodies — candy, chocolate, ice cream — was not often dispensed from their father's pockets — unless, of course, he had some left over from his bus fare.

There were two very good reasons for their father's financial state: indifference and design. Handling money did not scale high on Zvi's priority register. He was vitally interested in providing well for his family. The Lord was enabling him to do so. What he kept for himself was an afterthought. Whatever it was, it was always enough. In any event, Esther was a much better commissar than he would ever be. She knew what to do with money. She also knew what not to do with money. Zvi was, therefore, willing and wise to leave household matters in the hands of the woman who found her pattern in the realm of the *worthy woman* from Proverbs 31.

Other legends were two elders from the church. The first, Joseph Davidson, was a sedate, patriarchal figure who looked like one of the upper-class European Jews one saw in old pictures. His bearing and lifestyle held true to the image. Mr. Davidson was a man of substance and dignity — solid all the way through. That appraisal went beyond the man's appearance. His spiritual depth and character were reflected in his outward demeanor. The children would watch the Davidsons as they sat together at worship. If you sat close, you knew you would have to be on your best behavior. Mr. D. would not countenance any monkey business in church. A look was sufficient to restore and maintain order. But what children learned from Joseph Davidson was not cold severity; it was disciplining grace. They felt it in a way that would cause his memory to be cherished as a *legend* in the best sense of the term.

Uncle Nathan was another story completely. He was warm, friendly and drew children to him like a magnet. He laughed loud and loved fun — a good man for young children to have around. Unlike Joseph Davidson, who was an infrequent visitor, Uncle Nathan often dropped in for tea and talk. The joke was: "Good old Nathan, you can buy him with a slice of bread and a cup of tea." They could all testify of his fondness for both. He would sit in the kitchen, a tea cup on the table and a slice of bread, always unbuttered, in his hand. You could be sure that while he was there, the children would be close by. That's what set him apart. Uncle Nathan noticed the kids and cared very deeply about what God was doing in their lives. He demonstrated what Christian love and caring really was. (You'll remember that it was Uncle Nathan who risked his life under sniper fire to bring eggs to the family whose dad was off to war.) His life and lessons would stay with them. In a land where living for the Lord is sometimes pretty tough sledding, it is good to have an Uncle Nathan's charm and smile to light up your memory.

Nathan's wife came to Mendel at the conclusion of his baptism. Her husband had been with the Lord for some time. "You have made my Nathan so happy today. He is jumping up and down in Heaven!"

Like churches the world over, every member does not evidence the type of deportment which qualifies for *legend* status with those who need constructive Christian role models. The church the Weicherts attended was no exception. But as they began to mature, it would be people like Davidson and Nathan whose influence would be used by God to make a difference.

As Zvi's children were touched by sound, strong personalities, they were also affected by the traditions and festivals that make Israel unique. The feast of Esther (Purim) that comes each spring was an especially good time for small boys and girls.

Purim is for children, and during the spring festival it seems everyone in Israel becomes a child again. To be on the streets in Tel Aviv, when people are bopping other laughing people on the heads with squeaking plastic mallets, walking around in strange costumes and generally enjoying the merriment, is somewhat like walking down a midway at a carnival in small-town America. For a nation under perpetual stress and constantly living with hard realities, Purim is therapeutic.

Purim is celebrated by Jews the world over as the commemoration of Mordecai and Queen Esther's triumph over the infamous Haman and his plot to exterminate Jews throughout the Persian Empire. As is true with many Christian observances, it has been added to and altered over the centuries.

For religious Jews, the celebration is an annual reminder of God's protection for His people. In Hasidic literature, much is made of Purim as a day of friendship and joy and as a celebration of God at work, as an unseen hand, behind the scenes.

As one might expect, in the synagogues, the main feature in the commemoration is the reading of the Book of Esther. When what has been termed "the four verses of redemption" (2:5; 8:15,16; 10:3) are read, it is in a louder voice. The children, whenever the name of the hated Haman is heard from the text, make loud noises with Purim rattles, their voices, feet or anything appropriate to demonstrate their contempt for him. The noise is to blot out the name of Haman and "the memory of Amalek" — Haman was a descendant of Amalek, perpetual archenemy of ancient Israel.

It is customary at Purim to "send portions" to friends and give gifts to the poor. The rule is to send at least two portions of eatables to a friend and give a present of money to at least two poor men. A special meal of boiled beans and peas is eaten on Purim afternoon, which, it is said, is a reminder of the cereals eaten by Daniel when he was in the king's palace at Babylon. A favored treat is a special Purim pie, *hamantashen* (Haman's ears), eaten during the celebration.

For those who are less inclined toward the religious aspects of Purim, the Mardi Gras flavor gives the season its appeal. Practices adapted from the Italian carnival brought in the elaborate costuming seen today. In the spirit of Mardi Gras, excesses are indulged, among them some heavy drinking and allowing children to do pretty much as they please.

For the Weichert kids, it was Purim plays, dressing up and having good, clean fun.

There was the year when Ruthi showed her skills as a producer and director by preparing a Purim play for church families. She was also in charge of talent selection and coaching the participants in the program.

Her casting ability may have seemed a bit biased when Mendel appeared as Queen Esther, and Yona peered at the audience from the Mordecai costume. The play was a big hit and enhanced the spirit of joy and friendship reflected in the season.

As a child, Ruthi especially loved Purim. Her favorite role was that of Esther — beautiful and queenly — going about the business of being a heroine and deliverer of her people.

Costumes are important to little girls with such grand fantasies. She always fancied herself and her mother — the real, everyday Esther — in one of Jerusalem's finest shops, selecting the most elegant gown Purim would ever witness. But, as is so often true, reality fell a little short of her shimmering ideal. Esther was not the sort who frequented boutiques — even in her dreams. She leaned rather toward the clean and sensible. And spending hard money on a play dress to be worn for a day or two did not fall within the perimeters of *sensible.*

"This year, it will be different," Esther told her daughter with expensive tastes.

"What will be different? Are we going into the city to buy me a Purim costume?"

Mother quickly dashed that prospect. "No, we are not. But I have been giving it a great deal of thought, and this year you will have the perfect costume."

"Can you please tell me — or better, show me — what it will be?"

"No, that would spoil all the fun. You'll just have to wait until Purim, then you will see."

Ruthi was a picture of anticipation when she bounded out of bed on Purim morning. Suspense had disrupted her thoughts for days on end. At last, she would find out just what her mother's idea of a "best yet" costume was.

"Stand still," Esther instructed as she began to create. She worked deliberately over her impatient daughter, like a master craftsman on some great project. First, an immaculate white shirt, open at the collar. Then, she slipped her into a black suit — it turned out to be one of Zvi's. A pair of black shoes finished work on the lower level. "Now hold still, while I put this on your face." Ruthi could feel a pointed object being moved expertly over her upper lip. The production was finished when Esther wrapped her head with a bright red kafiyah and pulled a thick black cord to forehead level.

Esther stepped back for a survey, made a few adjustments here and there, then smiled approvingly. "Go look at yourself," she instructed. By this point, Ruthi was not so sure she really wanted to look.

Zvi's eldest child studied the image in the mirror. Her voice was composed as she spoke to her mother. "Would you tell me, please, just who, or what, I am supposed to be?"

"An Arab, of course," Esther replied.

"An Arab! I don't want to be an Arab! Beside, this is not an Arab costume. They wear long robes."

"No, old fashioned Arabs wear long robes, You are a modern Arab!"

As has happened before mirrors in every country the world over, after helpful mothers have lent their best efforts to clothe daughters appropriately, Esther watched her little girl burst into tears. It was, in fact, a terrific Purim costume. But the eyes of the foremost beholder could not see it that way. After all, how could a queen be comfortable in a scratchy black suit?

As things would have it, and before her girlish interest in pretty Purim costumes began to wane, Ruthi's dream came true. The source was consummately appropriate. Her grandmother, Esther's mother, sent her a special dress to wear to the wedding of an aunt from Persia — Esther's birthplace. This exotic garment — white, beautifully embroidered and flowing gracefully to the floor — had come from the land of her queen and Mordecai. It was one of those rare instances in life when a child's dream really did come true.

Next Purim, when the pretend Esther stepped from her door, she was, in bearing and appearance, every inch a queen. Oh, there were people who would try harder and spend a great deal in their attempts to achieve the ultimate, but the boutiques of Jerusalem or Tel Aviv would not produce one so elegant and happy as Zvi and Esther's daughter.

It was a fitting climax to Ruthi's play days. She was growing up. Pretend was giving way to life as it must be lived in Israel. Too soon, she would trade her beautiful Persian gown for olive drab Israeli army fatigues. It was the way sabra girls came of age.

CHAPTER NINE

FADING NUMBERS

In the years between the wars, Zvi and his family were enjoying the best of two worlds. They were living in the most exciting period in the history of their new nation. Maturing in the Lord, and watching Him work His will was even more fulfilling. But with all he was involved in with family, work and church, Zvi never forgot the people who had known the bad times in Europe. Most of his fellow survivors of the Holocaust had not yet found the peace they desperately needed. He wanted to do what he could to help them.

The dark numbers tattooed on pallid forearms have faded somewhat over the years — the memories haven't. Barbed wire — stench-filled barracks with narrow wooden beds — stomachs empty too long to complain anymore — minds dulled with hunger and fatigue — bodies wearing slatted rib cages and distended joints as creeping exhibitions of the horror — scowling guards and swastikas — guns — clubs — mud — moans — excrement — long lines of naked Jews waiting their turn in the "showers" — fumes from the furnaces — disease — atrocities too inhumane to describe crouching behind dark doors — rape — dissection — striped suits on grotesque hulks clutching electrified fences in quivering, self-induced death spasms — piles of human hair, shoes, gold-rimmed glasses, and clothes stacked before the "processing chambers," were all specters lurking much too close to the surface of their minds. They wanted to forget — most never could. Holocaust was not a dark historical pause for those who were there; it was an eternity of anguish compressed into a lifetime.

Many of them are gone now, and most in the world wish the Jews would stop reminding them — some even deny it ever happened. The remnant keeps vigil at the Holocaust memorial, Yad Vashem, in Jerusalem. Their representatives, most of them old, sit on benches, handkerchiefs to faces, outside the buildings housing grim artifacts of anti-Semitic insanity. Theirs is a presence which gives life and breath to the storied "weeping Jews of the diaspora" who provoked Byron to write:

The white dove hath her nest,
The fox his cave,
Mankind their country,
Israel but the grave.

In the great memorial shrine, an "eternal light" flickers over the entombed ashes of victims and lights the names of the extermination camps, which the world — like it or not — must remember: Auschwitz, Belzec, Chelmno, Kulmhof, Majdansk, Sobibor, Treblinka.

It is safe to say that all Holocaust victims bear lifelong scars of their ordeal. Some wounds are physical, as those inflicted by doctors at Dachau and Auschwitz in the name of "racial and medical research." Others are psychological — a scarring running far deeper than that brought about by knives and guns.

Zvi moved freely among them. His easy demeanor and obvious desire to help in any way he could soon taught survivors that this was a friend who could be trusted. Some encounters bore spiritual fruit; some did not — at least not immediately. Pathos and humor sometimes ran in the same stream as he lived with the people who wore the numbers. Shulman was a prime example.

Following Zvi's misadventure as a cook in the transit camp, he was directed toward a new barracks by the man in charge of placement.

"The only place we have for you now is with a man named Shulman. He's much older than you and, I must warn you, is an odd sort of fellow. Maybe it's because he spent so much time in concentration camps. Be patient with him and try to get along the best you can.

"I'm sorry we can't place you with someone nearer your age. If something opens up, I'll let you know."

"Well, at least it is a place to lay my head at night," Zvi said, as he went looking for his new quarters.

Shulman lived up to what he had been told to expect — he was an odd sort. Zvi judged him to be about sixty. He was short in stature and wore glasses so thick it was hard to believe his nose could support them. The face was round and not the most appealing Zvi had looked upon. "Oi," he thought, "if I had to choose between kissing that face and a monkey, I wouldn't think twice — it would be the monkey!"

His host didn't give him much time to indulge in frivolous humor. Shulman laid down the law.

"I will tell you now that I don't like the idea of having anyone living here with me. But since I have no choice in the matter, you will have to keep some rules. The first one is this: you cannot bring your friends here. I will not permit it. And I want this place kept clean. Furthermore, you are to leave my things alone. Don't touch anything that belongs to me."

"You don't have to worry," Zvi assured him, "I like things clean too. And I will respect your wishes about having my friends in while you are at home. Your belongings will be safe, and I promise to do what I can to help with what needs to be done."

It was soon obvious that Shulman had not completely shaken the lifestyle of the concentration camp. He was secretive and suspicious. Often, after they had eaten the evening meal, Zvi would see him slipping uneaten pieces of bread under his pillow. Every nook and cranny in the place seemed to be stuffed with packages. He recognized them as parcels of clothing sent into the camp by various relief agencies around the world. This clothing was to be distributed, without charge, to any one who needed it. Contrary to the established rules of distribution, Shulman had been gathering them up and building a carefully guarded hoard. Periodically, he would run checks on his goods to see that everything was still in place.

Living arrangements under these conditions were tolerable, if not exactly what one could call congenial. Absence helped, so Zvi spent much of his time away, and his housemate often ambled around the camp talking with people who were nearer his age and interests.

Shulman was away on a ramble when some of Zvi's friends dropped by to invite him along on a trip into town. While they were waiting for him, a young fellow remarked about all of the clothing packages in the place. "These are supposed to be given away," he said. "What are they doing here?"

"It is Shulman's hobby," Zvi laughed. "He just picks them up and stuffs them away."

"Well let's have a look and see what's inside some of them," his inquisitive visitor said.

He liked what he found much better than what he was wearing, so he helped himself, as did some of the others, and replaced the garments they had taken with their castoffs. It was, indeed, a better dressed company of youths who walked to Jerusalem that afternoon.

What had been good fun for them, however, was no laughing matter to Zvi's elder. "You are a thief," he shouted, trembling with anger. "I knew your being here was no good. Get out! Get out of my sight, and don't come back."

"That would be all right with me," Zvi replied, trying to remain calm, "but, you see, I have no place else to go."

"Then I will call the police and have you arrested. They will give you a place to stay."

"No," Zvi countered, "I don't think you should call the police. You know as well as I that those clothes are not to be kept as you are doing. They are to be distributed to whoever needs them. They don't belong to you or me, and the police won't like what they see if they come here."

Shulman knew he was right and said no more. The two lived with an uneasy truce from that point on. But, as things would have it, the cease-fire was not long-lived.

The old man's snoring was piercing the night's tranquility, when Zvi was awakened by a thirst which needed to be extinguished. There was no electricity in the place, and Zvi, not wanting to disturb his irritable elder, scorned a lamp and groped around in the dark for what he needed. Hands moved over the table until one bumped a glass that was partially filled with water. Zvi flipped the contents out the open window, filled it from the pail on the table, had his drink and went back to bed.

A storm of vindictives broke over him at about 6:00 in the morning. Shulman's wrathful verbal assault after the clothing incident seemed like a light warm-up compared to what he was dishing out now. When Zvi sat up on his bed and looked at the old man, he was certain that he had gone completely mad. He was going on in an uncontrollable rage about what Zvi had done to him and not to think he was going to get away with it this time. Further complicating the early hour, disjointed phrases and high-pitched passion was the fact that words were coming through severely puckered lips, which were emitting strange whistling noises. The object of Shulman's wrath had no earthly idea what this was all about or if — and it seemed an open question at the moment — his accuser was still sane.

Zvi injected a question at a break for breath. "But what have I done to you?"

"You know very well what you have done to me, you thief. My teeth! You stole my teeth during the night! What have you done with them?"

A deep wave of nausea momentarily blocked out the man's words. That partially filled glass had contained the article that kept Shulman's mouth in business. Zvi had thrown his teeth out the window. But worse, far worse to Zvi's mind than a missing upper plate, was what had transpired immediately following that ill-fated act — he drank from the glass bearing the old man's teeth! For a few distressing moments, he felt as though he were about to lose more than Shulman had.

The whole thing was, of course, preposterous. At his age, Zvi had a full set of his own teeth. And where would one find a customer for a used set of teeth — especially in the middle of the night? The irrational tirade reflected the residual imbalance deposited during his time behind the wire. He would never get over it.

Unfortunately, a search for the missing plate was futile, and Shulman was forced to gum it until a replacement set could be made — free of charge.

The placement officer had been correct when he offered reservations about the arrangement. It wasn't difficult to see that this was not going to work out. It was Shulman himself who decided to make the break.

"I'm moving out," he informed Zvi.

"But where will you go?"

"Oh, I have a place. I am moving in with a friend of mine. We are the same age, so this will be a much better arrangement for both of us."

The part of the man that was showing during their conversation that day was the pre-concentration camp Shulman. He was a good man, but a man so deeply scarred that one had trouble finding him beneath the rubble. The summary tragedy of what Hitler did to survivors of the Holocaust was not just what he took away, though that was unspeakably horrible, it was what he left them to live with for the rest of their natural lives.

Zvi, as one who had been there, was fully aware of this and had a deep desire to reach out to him. He hadn't been a believer long himself, but he knew that Shulman needed what he had found in the Lord. But how to approach him, and what to say — those were the questions. Zvi asked the Lord for some appropriate words to give the man before they parted. The Lord supplied them.

"You tell me that you have found a friend with whom to live. I am very happy for you. It will be good for you to have someone your own age with whom you can live and talk.

"I want you to know that I, too, have found a friend with whom to live. He is here with me all the time. When I came to Israel, I was alone like you. All my family was lost, and, in another way, I was lost too. I wondered what I had to live for. Then I came to know the Lord Jesus Christ as my Savior. When I did, I found the friend I needed. I hope that one day you can find Him too."

It was a short, simple witness for the Lord Jesus — nothing detailed or profoundly theological, just one heart telling another that there is a friend who, in love and grace, sees through the scars and reaches out to us with His peace.

Shulman listened. Zvi hoped he understood. They parted company to move away to very different personal worlds. Only eternity will tell us if the old man with Hitler's tattoo found a new friend in the Lord Jesus.

It was different with Leo.

His nervousness caught Zvi's eye. The man worked in quick, jerky little movements. During idle moments, he paced around the construction site puffing on one cigarette after another.

One day during their lunch break, Zvi motioned him over. "Come, sit down, let's eat together."

His fellow worker hunkered down beside him, munched a bit of food, then lit another cigarette.

"I'm curious," Zvi began, "I don't think I've ever seen a person smoke more cigarettes in a day than you do. How many packs do you put away?"

"Four or five," he answered.

"Well, if you don't mind some friendly advice, you had better cut down or you'll wind up with emphysema, and that's a hard way to live and die."

His companion bristled. "If you only knew what I've been through in my life, you wouldn't be so smart and quick to pass out advice." With that he sauntered off to another corner of the job site.

Of course, Zvi didn't know what his irritated comrade had been through. But he drew some general conclusions when he noticed the blue numbers tattooed on his arm.

Later in the day, Zvi approached the man with a grin. "I'm sorry if I offended you. I didn't mean to hurt your feelings.

"I'll tell you what, why don't you and your family come over on Shabbat. My wife will prepare a nice meal for us, and our families can get acquainted."

Leo seemed eager to accept Zvi's invitation. The next Saturday afternoon, after introductions were made all around, the families sat down to enjoy one of Esther's culinary masterpieces.

After dinner, the two men took a walk and shared some quiet conversation. His new friend began to talk freely. Clearly, there was some burden he wanted to unload.

"You asked me why I chain smoke on the job the other day. Well, I'm going to tell you. Then I want you to answer a question yourself: If you had experienced what I have, would you be any different?"

"Good," Zvi replied, "I would like to hear your story."

"As a young man — it seems so long ago now — I had a beautiful wife and a healthy baby boy. We had a good life from my trade as a cabinetmaker. Life couldn't have been better for us.

"Then came the war, and, as you know, we Jews were in trouble. Eventually, we were picked up by the Germans and sent to Auschwitz.

"I will never forget the smell of the boxcar we rode in to the concentration camp — maybe that's why I smoke so much. For days we were locked inside. People had no food, and some were suffocating for lack of air. I pushed us into a little space near the door of the car so at least we could get enough air through the cracks to survive.

"The stink from body wastes and the people, alive and dead, were unbearable. We were, of course, in no position to alter our circumstances.

"When we finally got to the camp, the door was opened, and we were herded off like so many starving cattle.

"I was relieved. At least, I thought, we are still alive and together. But hunger was eating at our guts, and I knew we must have something to eat soon.

"After a while, I saw a cart loaded with potatoes passing nearby on the way to the kitchen. I couldn't resist. I quickly grabbed one — only one — and stuck it under my coat. Unfortunately, a guard saw me do it.

" 'We don't like thieves here,' I was told. 'When we catch them, we make examples of them. Take this shovel and dig a hole over there.' I did as I was told. When I was finished, the guard shouted at me. 'Now get in!'

"I thought they were going to bury me alive. But when the dirt was up to my neck, they stopped kicking it in on me.

"We were all at Auschwitz for only one purpose: to die. But it was even more grotesque to think that these animals were going to play games with us while we did.

"I stayed there for about 24 hours with my head sticking out of the ground. Some of the guards even came over and kicked it like a soccer ball as they walked by.

"Now I was sure that I would never get out of that hole alive, and I didn't really care. I began hallucinating — I couldn't remember — I was waiting for death.

"The sight of my wife and boy snapped me out of it. At first I thought I was dreaming. But, no, there they were standing above me. Maybe, after all, I told myself, there was a small spark of humanity in this awful place.

"I was crazy to even think such a thing. A big guard came over and took our baby — he was only a year old — away from my wife. Another guard, who had a rifle with a long bayonet attached, was standing nearby.

" 'Here, see if you can catch this,' he said, and threw my boy into the air. The guard caught him on his bayonet.

"My wife screamed, and I struggled with all my might to free myself. She ran toward the baby — reaching out for him. They knocked her down, and as she was trying to get up they shot her dead before my eyes.

"It was like my life ended too. I wasn't physically dead, but I wasn't alive either. The Germans, I would soon learn, had no intention of extending that favor to me. For the moment, at least, they had need of me.

"I was registered as a carpenter, and when they dug me up I was put to work on a building detail.

"I worked like a mechanical man. Time after time I could see them again — hear the gun. My only thought was: I wish they would have shot me too."

Leo looked at Zvi intently. "Do you understand now why I can't sit still; why I smoke so much?"

Zvi had heard it all before, not the same gruesome details perhaps, but the same story of death and despair. Unknown to his friend, he had seen it — lived it. And for years he had spent a great deal of his time going in and out among the aging people who bore the faded blue numbers.

"Now I will tell you just how much I understand what you went through. For you, all this started when you were 26 years old. For me, in Warsaw, the horror came when I was only 10. I was like a little cat surrounded by a thousand dogs — and so I lived during the war."

For two hours Zvi talked about his own experiences. The man listened and wept as he began to understand that Zvi represented much more than an attentive ear. He was a comrade in suffering who knew — really knew — how it had been. The experience forged a friendship which would last until Leo died a number of years later.

Now the door was open for Zvi to tell his friend how to find a new beginning. Patiently, at every opportunity, he unfolded the story of what he himself had found in the Lord.

Zvi's faithful witness and God's power ultimately brought the man, who had wished himself dead, back from his spiritual grave — he came to know Christ as his Savior. As a result, his children by a second marriage were placed in a school operated by Christians. One by one, they too became believers.

Everything changed for Leo after he came to the Lord. Oh, the blue number was still there. But it was no longer the only story of his life. It was now only a fading memory for the carpenter from Europe.

One day, when they were working together, Zvi had a question for his friend. "Leo, I notice that you aren't smoking today. What has happened?"

"Believe me, Zvi, only the Lord could have taken the cigarettes away. He has, and I thank Him for doing it.

"And it's not just the cigarettes — this was only a small thing. He has brought me out from my troubles. Best of all, I know where I'm going when all this is over."

Leo's and Shulman's stories are only two of thousands that could be told by Holocaust survivors. Sadly, they are not often stories of spiritual triumph. But for Zvi and those few other Jewish believers who outlasted Europe's trauma, the fires of suffering have created unique opportunities; for while Holocaust victims will sometimes, almost grudgingly and in guarded terms, discuss their trials with a few who ask, they will open their mouths and hearts to those who shared their ordeal. Thus, the opportunity to bring the light of the gospel is presented — dimly at first, because their night has been so dark. But for this segment of Jewry's precious "remnant," the light increases until it illuminates eternity and shows the way home!

CHAPTER TEN

A MEAT GRINDER WAR

"Howbeit on the tenth day of this seventh month is the day of atonement; there shall be a holy convocation unto you, and ye shall afflict your souls; and ye shall bring an offering made by fire unto the Lord" (Lev. 23:27, Masoretic Text).

Yom Kippur is a day for the collective "afflicting of soul" for world Jewry. Little did Israelis who went quietly to their synagogues for early services on the Day of Atonement in October, 1973 realize the intensity of the "offering by fire" that was just hours away. Their offering would not be a lamb sacrificed "unto the Lord" on the great altar at the Temple. Israel's finest and bravest young men were about to be offered by fire on the altar of national survival.

In the crucible of affliction which lay ahead, many a Jewish soldier would question the *haftarah* reading for Yom Kippur which promised: "He will turn again; he will have compassion upon us; he will subdue our iniquities; and thou wilt cast all their sins into the depths of the sea. Thou wilt perform the truth to Jacob, and the mercy to Abraham, which thou hast sworn unto our fathers from the days of old" (Mic. 7:19-20). To Israelis, those wonderful words of promise seemed light years removed from anything they were to experience in the Yom Kippur War.

The war that disrupted the most solemn commemoration on the Jewish religious calendar also held religious overtones for their Arab attackers. Arabs reasoned that Israel would not expect them to attack during the month of Ramadan (a month of Arab fasting). Furthermore, the 6th of October had special meaning to Arabs, because it corresponded, according to the Moslem calendar, with the day on which the Prophet Mohammed began preparations for the battle of Badr — a battle which opened the door to the capture of Mecca and the spreading of Islam. Accordingly, the code name "Operation Badr" (lightning) was given to the operation.

79

The Yom Kippur War, as a military collision, was the cruelest of all confrontations between Israel and her enemies — a fact precisely in line with Egyptian planning. Egypt knew that Israeli military manpower limitations would not permit heavy losses of life. In terms of Israeli lives lost, recent conflicts had not been unduly expensive: Sinai Campaign (1956), 200 casualties; Six-Day War (1967), 800; War of Attrition (1968-70), 400. The highest Arab priority, as in other wars, was the annihilation of Israel. Short of that fanciful dream being accomplished, Syria and the Egyptians wanted Israel to pay far more than she could afford in manpower, morale and economic security. Egyptian War Minister and Commander-in-Chief, General Ahmed Ismail, concluded, "Our strike should be the strongest we can deal. We must 'chop the Israelis up.' " Egypt's Chief of Staff, General Shazli, phrased it in a forebodingly terse term: it will be "a meat grinder war."

The ensuing Arab attack, which inexplicably caught Israel by surprise, did indeed, for a few days, put Israel into Shazli's "meat grinder." But, as had been the case in each of Israel's modern wars, the grinder ultimately turned to mangle the Egyptians and Syrians. Once again, Mohammed's finest were put to flight by Jehovah's chosen few — Israel turned almost certain defeat into a stunning victory.

But in the process of achieving victory, Israel had been badly mauled by her adversaries. In just 18 days, 2,522 young men lost their lives while thousands more suffered combat wounds.

Military considerations aside, the Yom Kippur War was a major turning point in the modern history of the Middle East. The decisive Six-Day War had been the high-water mark for Jews who had returned to Zion with such high hopes. The very euphoria enveloping the sweeping victory over the Arabs and the climactic reunification of Jerusalem helped set the stage for the near disaster of Yom Kippur. The Arabs saw the overconfidence produced by Israel's self-indulgent euphoria as a weapon in their hands. Egyptian General Ismail commented to this effect by saying, "He [Israel] is, moreover, an enemy who suffers the evils of wanton conceit." Israel learned the hard way that conceit could be a deadly companion.

For Israel and Arabs alike, Yom Kippur was an opening and closing of doors. Arabs, once again, saw their crushing defeat as a victory of sorts. Egyptian and Syrian achievements in the first days of war were, in their eyes, proof that Israel had lost her deterrent power. Arab leaders were led to conclude that, with larger quantities of modern weapons and more intensive preparation for the next round, they might solve the Middle East problem by military rather than diplomatic means. Their attitude opened the door for the emergence of militant Palestinian actions — actions which would eventually create the quagmire in Lebanon. Of equal, or even greater importance, was the decision by some former allies to reassess commitments to Israel in the wake of Arab inclinations to use their oil as a weapon of war.

Israelis saw some doors close on Yom Kippur in 1973. Obviously, their grandiose feelings of military invincibility had deserted them. And while Jews have, out of brutal necessity, always been realists, there were grave questions about how far their "friends" would go in supporting Israel's right to survive if pocketbooks were threatened. Some, as in the case of Western Europe, Japan and several African nations, had headed for the door as soon as their oil supplies were threatened. Of greater monument to the people of Israel was the fact that this war saw Zionist idealism begin to wane. That super-confidence that "the dream" could be achieved through Jewish ingenuity and effort had become gravely suspect. The question which only time could answer was: "Is the Zionist dream of living in peace and security in the land of our fathers, after all, obtainable?" Many were beginning to wonder.

In the final analysis, the war's legacy settled mainly in the psychological and emotional residual left in the population of Israel by the conflict. The key question was, after all, essentially religious and messianic. And from a completely different perspective, it brought the nation back to the fundamental elements of the Day of Atonement with which they had been involved when so rudely interrupted only days before. Then it had been largely a religious ceremony — one taking place in an environment of confidence and security. Now, with confidence shattered and security badly shaken, it was clearly time for some Israelis to begin to look beyond themselves and the nation for personal assurance of peace with God and confidence that, whatever the future held for Israel, they could personally know better days. Some Israelis were finally beginning to ask the right questions, and there were a few among them who could give them the right answers. Zvi Weichert was one of them.

Zvi awakened on the morning of Yom Kippur expecting to spend a quiet day in company with family and friends. He was surprised to hear what sounded to him like a radio playing faintly in the distance. "Playing a radio on Yom Kippur," he said to himself, "whoever it is, must be out of his mind. He could get rocks on his head in a hurry."

As he was dressing, he casually looked out into the street. More people were moving about than one would expect to see at this hour on the Day of Atonement. Here and there, he could see cars moving slowly through the streets. That was a sure sign something was up. He reached for the radio and turned it on. Esther rushed from the bedroom when she heard sounds coming from the radio. "Zvi, Zvi," she warned. "Turn off the radio. Did you forget today is Yom Kippur? If anyone hears it, they will be over here making trouble for us."

Her voice barely penetrated. Word was out that it was apparent Egypt and Syria were preparing for war. A partial call-up of reserve forces had already begun.

At 4:30 that morning, the High Command had concluded that the enemy actually intended to attack. The decision against a preemptive assault was made, and the limited call-up of reserves began. It was much later in the morning (9:30) when the call for total mobilization of forces was issued. (The Egyptians and Syrians launched simultaneous attacks at 2:00 in the afternoon.)

Zvi watched as neighbors were being picked up and whisked off to duty stations. A friend called to him as he was leaving his house. "Hey Zvi! You had better enjoy the holiday quick. The guys with your invitation can't be far behind." The scene was all too familiar to Zvi, Esther and the children. Soon the men would come with the red call-up card and ask him to sign the verification that he had been officially notified. Accordingly, he would get his things together, say a quick good-by, and leave them standing in the doorway, stretching their necks to watch him until he was out of sight.

This time it turned out to be a bit different. "You must come with us immediately," he was told. There was urgency bordering on distress in their voices. If war was imminent, they knew Israel was up against it, and they all had their work cut out for them. They could only hope it was not too little too late.

When Zvi and his unit reached the assembly area from which troops would be deployed, there seemed to be an air of confusion totally untypical of the IDF. The men waited for their weapons, but none were delivered. They spent the first night without arms and wondering when they would be supplied. "We're sitting ducks," one soldier complained. "As things stand now, a few Arabs could wipe out a regiment."

That fear was quieted with the arrival of supplies, and the men were off to save the nation once again. For Zvi and his fellow sappers, it was again wartime musical chairs. Up to the Golan to plant mines; down to the Sinai on the same urgent mission; then off to the Jordan to place a protective buffer between Israel and the Jordanians, who were mobilized as a diversion. Arabs wanted Israel to be concerned on three fronts, so they would be able to concentrate totally on Syrian and Egyptian forces.

Heat was oppressive along the Jordan, and soldiers, who went days without sleep, were tormented by the threat of dehydration that drained precious energy from their exhausted bodies.

Israel's plight demanded heroism and sacrifices which went far beyond those normally expected in the dreaded game men call war. Zvi came very near making the ultimate sacrifice on the Golan Heights. The Syrian onslaught there had been all but irresistible. One hundred MIG-17 fighters led the assault across the Golan. Next, Syrian artillerymen "walked" a curtain of fire toward the squadrons of Israeli tanks assembling at their firing stations. Behind the shelling, 700 Syrian tanks rolled to the attack against Israel's skeleton force. Syrians were entertaining visions of sipping tea in Tiberias. Israelis worked frantically to stop them.

"We need mines here quickly," Zvi was told. The area was swept by intense fire, but waiting for a more propitious moment was not an option open to Jewish commanders. "Don't worry. We will provide cover for you." Zvi went about his work with the total concentration his occupation demanded. Only when he had managed to finish his job unscathed did he notice that he was completely alone. His unit had gone about other business and left him to finish his work unattended. He had some words for his commanding officer when he later found his unit. "You made a promise you didn't keep," Zvi complained with obvious justification. "Exposed as I was, I could have been killed."

His officer understood his frustration. "In this fight," the man answered, "one man cannot be our first priority. Our job now is to save the state of Israel." Zvi's understanding nod mirrored the larger situation. Every soldier had to be considered expendable; Israel must survive. Zvi had, in fact, been well-covered while he was about his dangerous occupation: The Lord's hand of protection was covering His chosen vessel.

Strange turns of war — events which remain unexplained fully to this day — assured Zvi that this war had larger ramifications than man could manipulate with tanks and missiles. Both Egypt and Syria, when they appeared to have complete victory in their grasp, stopped dead in their tracks. Humanly speaking, it was a fatal blunder. With the passing of each irresolute hour, the Arabs were delivering time to their Jewish foes — time to get men to the field, time to regroup, time to formulate strategy, time to strike back, time for Jews to wonder why they were granted enough time to assure their survival. "Who gave us time? And why?"

Those questions, and the somber realities of war, wiped the smiles from the faces of Jewish combatants. When there was time for reflection, despondent young men began to seek some answers.

"Why do you think the Egyptians stopped?" a swarthy sabra asked Zvi while they were sitting together. "I must believe two things," Zvi replied. "First, God has allowed us to be punished because we have been proud and believed that we always win because we are great fighters — so strong. Second, while God has punished us, He has also preserved us. We are, after all, a people who cannot be destroyed. And why is this? It is as it says in the Bible: 'thou shouldest be my servant...I will also give thee for a light to the nations' [Isa. 49:6]. Someday it will be so. We are being perserved to do this. For too long we have believed that our success was from our own strength. I tell you that is wrong. Think seriously about all our wars. In '48, we should not have won, but we did; '67 was the same. We were so few, they were so many, but it looked so easy for us to defeat them. Now there is a good lesson for us, if we will only take it to our hearts. We almost lost — yes, we were punished — but, somehow, we were saved. That 'somehow' was always God watching over us. There is no other reasonable explanation." Zvi's fellow soldier had heard some points to ponder.

Israelis who were not acquainted with the Scriptures seemed to be getting at least some of the message. The mood after the Six-Day War had been, almost universally: "Look what we did in our power." By 1973, that mood had been swept away. Now many of Zvi's companions were shaken to the point of asking themselves what — or who — was responsible for this victory. They were hard pressed to say, "We did it."

As a result, the Bible became required reading for serious inquirers. Zvi came back to his tent one day to find a sergeant on his cot reading Zvi's Bible. He made a habit of leaving it out where it could be seen hoping someone might become curious and pick it up. Zvi had attempted to share his witness with this man on several occasions before the war. Each time he had met with a stone wall. The sergeant was very outspoken in telling Zvi he wanted nothing to do with such conversations. Now, not only was he reading the Bible, but he was having conversations with Zvi about what he read. His sergeant friend also became an eager participant in discussions on the Bible and religion provoked by what they had all been through.

The sergeant was not the exception. For the first time in his experience in the Israeli Defense Force, men were asking him to get them Bibles. A supply he brought back after a brief visit home was soon gone. "When you leave the tent for work," he suggested, "leave the Bible behind so others can read while they are off duty." It was a stimulating sight to the eyes of a man who had witnessed so earnestly and prayed so faithfully for God to open the eyes of his comrades to spiritual truth. Zvi took stock of the men serving with him and estimated that at least 40% were reading Bibles in the aftermath of Yom Kippur. Not all, however, were pleased by his efforts.

"Let me see one of those Bibles." The request came from a bearded Orthodox soldier.

"Certainly," Zvi answered, and handed the man a copy.

As the man thumbed through the Book, a frown began to wrinkle his forehead. "It is as I thought. This Bible has the New Testament. What do you think you are doing bringing such poison here among Jews?"

Before Zvi could answer, another soldier solved the problem. "This Book may bother you," he said, "but it is not a problem for me. Here, give it to me. I will read it."

In other times, the incident would have precipitated an unpleasant scene. But now it seemed — after all they had endured — there wasn't much heart for another fight.

It was not too much to say that out of what was a terrible time for the country, there was blessing from the Lord. At least for awhile, He had the attention of many in the nation. Oh, they had not come all the way — although, thank God, some had. But it was as though Israel had taken a few halting steps toward Him — short steps to be sure, but, nonetheless, the sobering effects of Yom Kippur would open great doors of opportunity to witness of His power in Messiah for those who really knew God.

Zvi served for 73 days before he was finally sent home. As he started the trek toward Ir Ganim, like his nation, he was a troubled man — but not for the same reasons. He faced returning home to his faithful wife and four expectant children without a shekel in his pocket. How strange it seemed to experience such a sudden and dramatic change in priorities. During the war he was afforded virtually no time for such thoughts. Now it was the foremost consideration in his life. Saving the nation had given way to facing the family. What would he do?

He decided to go by his place of employment and talk to them about his situation. Everyone was smiling when he walked through the door. "Zvi," his boss called out, "we are so happy to see you. Come, sit down, let's talk about getting back to work."

"Yes, I'm happy to see you too. It will be good to get back to our work after the job I've been doing for the past couple of months. At the moment, I have a problem. I'm going home, and I don't have any money to take to my family."

"I'm sorry to have to tell you this," his boss said in a very serious tone, "but, my friend, you do not have a problem."

Zvi answered with a bit of perplexity in his voice. "What is this, 'I don't have a problem'?"

"You see, Zvi, while you were fighting for us, we were thinking of you. Here is a check for a full two months work. And for good measure, we have thrown in another half-month's pay as a bonus!" Before Zvi could say thanks, the man continued, "And that is not all. Over there in the corner is a big box of chocolate and presents for you to take home to the children. They have been prepared for all our men who went to the war. Take it. Go home to your family and enjoy."

Someone, a frequent traveler no doubt, once said: "Going home makes being away worth it!" Zvi may not have known the phrase, but, as a man who loved his family as much as a man can, he shared a full portion of the sentiment.

"It's abba," Mendel shouted at the top of his lungs, and promptly fell down three steps in his effort to be first to tackle his father. They were all on him in a flash. Ruthi and Esther covered him with kisses. Mendel and Yona hugged and wrestled, while Eli rode his shoulders like a conquering Roman. And, yes, in a way only soldiers who survive the fray can know, going home was worth it.

Zvi soaked up a full ten minutes of uninterrupted adoration. Then the children turned their focus of attention to the mysterious package. It was time for the triumphant soldier to become Abba the Distributor and Arbitrator. He was, once again, back to being abba with a small 'a' — and that was the way he liked it best. And Esther? She didn't get much from the box. The candy went to the kids; the check — and Zvi — went to Esther. She was quite willing to settle for that.

CHAPTER ELEVEN

THE HAPPIEST DAY

"And Moses said unto the people, Remember this day, in which ye came out from Egypt, out of the house of bondage; for by strength of hand the LORD brought you out from this place...And thou shalt show thy son in that day, saying, This is done because of that which the LORD did for me when I came forth out of Egypt" (Ex. 13:3,8).

There is a sense of immediacy about the Passover season in Israel. This is perfectly understandable because participants there are in close geographical proximity to the places where the scenes were played in the first festive celebration. One hundred fifty miles to the east, beyond the sands of the Sinai, lays Egypt, the land where Israel lived out her days of debilitating slavery. Abraham's sons and daughters passed long years of suffering among the dunes and desert winds known so well to modern descendants of those ancient pilgrims. Finally, Israel had seized the dream reckoned by the promise: "And he brought us out from there, that he might bring us in, to give us the land which he sware to give unto our fathers" (Dt. 6:23). Those who in that Promised Land lift their memorial glasses in the true spirit of Passover can justifiably feel the ties binding them to Israel's history and the faithful God who performs what He promises.

Twentieth-century Israelis are a witness to the awesome aspects of their enduring bond to Jehovah and reflect a modern parallel to the days of Moses and the patriarchs. For two thousand years, their forefathers wandered in the desert places of a hostile world. Often enslaved by hard taskmasters, they bled out the centuries and millennia weeping to be home and crying, "Next year in Jerusalem!" As in Pharaoh's Egypt, the nations finally lost their grip, and from deep chasms of persecution men like Herzl raised the cry, "Let my people go!" And they came out of the nations to enter into their land. Emaciated masses from a hundred countries crossed over on their journey home. But just as it had been with Joshua, Canaan was not a place of rest and quietude — *entering in* equalled struggle and war. So, when sons and daughters of their illustrious forebears read Haggadah declarations that "we are no more slaves, but free people," they recline on Passover pillows with weapons of war close at hand to insure that the promise remains a reality.

Hebrew Christians retain those links with biblical origins and historical actualities. But for them, there is so much more. Behind all of the events depicted and remembered in Passover, there are prophecy, providence, fulfillment and shadows of a future destiny.

Zvi's Jerusalem is the place where Jesus and His disciples lived out the events of the consummating Passover. Jerusalemites routinely walk over the streets and sites where it all came to pass. It is the Jerusalem where huddled groups of believers met around tables in remembrance of Him as forces dedicated to their extinction vowed that every remembrance of the Nazarene would be quickly eradicated. Nearly two thousand years later, they are still there — and in growing numbers. And while living every day amid such sacred scenes may tend to become part of the routine business of living, they are all freshened again by the spring breezes of Passover.

The first Passover Zvi and his family spent in their new home was rather a symbolic experience. Ir Ganim was a place of crowded, narrow streets, cramped houses and the problems living in such situations can create. This latest move took them into an area near the section where Zvi had lived as a newcomer to the city after the War of Independence.

So many things were different from life in Ir Ganim. This place didn't have the look of just having grown up of its own accord. It was a new, planned housing area. Ample space, lots of good places for the children to play, wide streets and flower-lined walks — you could smell spring in this place.

And the view! The area offered a spectacular panorama of Jerusalem. One could look right up the convergence of the Kidron and Hinnon valleys, over Mount Zion to the stately walls of the Old City and on to the golden Dome of the Rock. Seeing the city from that spot at night is a breathtaking experience. The children could look out a window across the shepherds fields and on down to Bethlehem. From a vantage point behind the house, the haze-covered Dead Sea rests in full view. In between, the light brown hills of the Judean wilderness run like a soft carpet down to the sea. Moab's silent mountains occupy the skyline on the other side of the Jordan River. Beyond them is Hussein's Jordan. Herod's palace-fortress, Herodium, sticks up out of the desert like a chopped-off, inverted ice cream cone. The man so violently opposed to the Christ who could move mountains literally built one for himself there in the desert.

As it was with Israel's initial Passover, this was a new *beginning* for Zvi and his family. Pesach was a fitting setting for celebrating the event. For the kids, this was "the happiest day of the year." But it was not just one day on the Weichert calendar. Preparations began a month in advance of the festive occasion with Esther's dismantling of the premises in a relentless search for anything remotely resembling dirt. Ruthi was her first mate on the spring cleaning detail. To her childish mind, it all seemed so unnecessary, boring and just plain wearing on a person's body. The worst thing was wondering if this was ever going to end. She was firm in her conviction that Passover was "the happiest day of the year." That sentiment, however, did not cover the month which preceded the big day.

Pesach provided Esther with her brightest opportunity to do justice to preparing a meal. She was not particular about how many guests came through the door — the more people, the greater satisfaction in a job well done. Her children would rise up to call her blessed just remembering the aromas that floated from the kitchen. The sharp smell of horseradish (bitter herbs) was tempered by that of fresh cut greens, fruits, cinnamon and other pungent spices. Bubbling pots of dumplings and other sumptuous dishes combined to provide pleasantries for the nostrils. Perhaps the most appealing in tempting young appetites toward inordinate desire was the smell of *teyglekh* (honey cakes) browning in the oven.

The table itself was something to behold. The heavy, sparkling white tablecloth was graced by shining new dishes — the very best family resources could provide. Deep goblets, filled with blood red fruit of the vine, cast scarlet shadows down on the linen. Platters were stacked high with food in such abundance that the children stood in wide-eyed amazement at their mother's handiwork. Passover greens — it seemed every green vegetable grown — were richly contrasted against the beautiful silver plate on which they had been carefully arranged. An ornate Passover plate held the representative shank bone, egg, bitter herbs and haroseth. A three-tiered matzo dish held its precious ceremonial wafers with proper dignity. And, just like every year they could remember, there was the prettiest goblet of all — filled to the brim — in the exalted position of "the Cup of Elijah." Stately candles sent a flickering, soft aura to light the room and beam a sort of regal affirmation of the children's belief that this was, indeed, the happiest of days.

Zvi practiced an *open door* policy at Passover. Literally anybody who wished to come was welcomed — relative, friend or stranger. Special care was taken to invite singles and people who had no family with whom they could share the celebration. Friends from the church were always present. But among the great spectacles of Pesach was to see faces at the table completely unknown to anyone in the family — they just decided to come, and so they did. It was not unusual for as many as thirty people to gather with Zvi's family. He was happy that the Lord had provided a place large enough to accommodate the crowds.

When all were seated, and he began the *seder* service, Zvi always found himself looking out on a *mixed multitude.* Many were, of course, believers. But there were inevitably a number of unbelievers at the table as well. He was, therefore, presented with a prime opportunity to share Christ. Consequently, he had at his disposal a Passover Haggadah (a guidebook for the traditional Jewish *seder* ritual) and his Bible to expound how "Christ, our passover, is sacrificed for us" (1 Cor. 5:7).

There is probably no setting superior to Passover for bridging over to a clear and simple presentation of the gospel with Jewish people. Simply put, Christ is everywhere in the Pesach memorial. Even traditional ornaments of Judaism demonstrate this. For example, "Artwork on one Jewish *seder* dish features the Messiah entering Jerusalem on a donkey, led by Elijah blowing a ram's horn, while David is playing his harp" (*Encyclopedia Judaica*). The emblems on such a dish would give a golden opportunity to present both the suffering and reigning aspects of the Messiah's ministry toward us.

Zvi used tradition and truth to seize the moment for his Savior. As they moved through the ceremony, he selected statements and events consistent with biblical objectives. "Our fathers were enslaved in Egypt. On the night that the plague of the death of the firstborn came upon the Egyptians, Israel was spared because of the Passover lamb. They put the blood of the slain lamb on the doorposts and lintels of their houses, and when God saw the blood, He passed over and they were safe. Moses then led them out of Egypt and they began life as free people."

The kids were impressed with Zvi's practical comments on slavery and freedom. "Pesach was to show how people could pass from not believing, to believing — darkness to light — from being a slave to finding freedom in the Lord.

"We also learned that we should never forget who we are, or where we came from. No matter where we go, or how big we become, we are no better than anyone else. Always treat everybody with respect, and do your best to be good to everyone."

Jewish tradition arranged the matzo (unleavened bread) in such a way as to almost, in itself, preach Christ. Three matzos are stacked in a compartmented tray. As is done by Jews the world over, Zvi selected the middle matzo, broke it, wrapped it in a napkin and *hid* it. That broken matzo becomes the afikomen (literally: *I came*). At the conclusion of the *seder* meal, the wrapped half of the afikomen is unwrapped and comes forth to be broken to provide a portion for all to eat — everyone must partake. "Christ our Passover" is also "Christ our afikomen." He came to us as the second (middle) person of the Godhead three. He was broken for us on the cross; wrapped in graveclothes; *hidden* in a garden tomb in Jerusalem; brought forth in resurrection; and for two thousand years has been presented to Jew and Gentile alike as the One who will give eternal life to all those who will partake of Him. Many who sat at Zvi's table had never heard that news coming out of Jewry's most revered ceremony before.

His major emphasis, however, came straight from the divine Haggadah (his Bible), not Judaism's.

"We must understand that Pesach is not just a story of matzo and slavery. The lamb was the most important part of Pesach, and the lamb's blood had to be shed and applied. If it had not been so, none of them would have been saved.

"The lesson for us is this: We, everyone of us, were slaves. There is no way this kind of slave can free himself. Only God can show us the way. And He has. The Lord himself came to become the Lamb for you and for me. He shed His blood for us, so we can be free.

"Many of our Jewish people are saying, at this very moment, 'We are no longer slaves, we are free.' If they are only talking about the nation, this may be true in a sense. But if they are talking about the Lord, this is not true. If we receive the Lord, we are free. If we have not received the Lord, we are not free. It is as simple as that.

"My family and I, along with thousands and thousands of others, have received the Lord Jesus Christ as our Messiah and Savior. Now we can say, 'Once we were slaves, but now we are free.'

"It is possible to come together and have a wonderful time, as we are doing here tonight, go home and, in a matter of a few hours, forget what we have done.

"The main thing the Lord wants us to remember tonight is that we all can be free if we will receive the blood of the Lord."

Festivities continued long after the *seder* service was concluded and they had joined in singing the Hallel (Psalms 115-118). With bulging belt lines and merry hearts they sang and fellowshiped far into the night. The evening, which began around the table at about 7:00, would reluctantly conclude well after midnight.

As the children settled down in their beds, they reflected on the fact that this was certainly a night unlike all others. They couldn't wait for a year to pass so they could do it all again.

CHAPTER TWELVE

LET'S HEAR IT FOR THE CARTERS

Whan Jimmy Carter stepped off Air Force 1 at Lod International Airport outside Tel Aviv on March 10, 1979, he held high hopes for making history. He, along with his top aides, had already met with Egyptian President Anwar Sadat in Cairo to work on details of the peace plan Sadat declared had Egypt and Israel "on the verge of an agreement."

After days of exhaustive discussions, filled with soaring emotional highs and lows, the Israeli Cabinet approved the treaty by a 15-2 vote. On March 21st, the Knesset overwhelmingly ratified the decision. On March 26th, President Sadat and Prime Minister Menachem Begin signed the historic treaty at a White House ceremony in Washington, D.C. as President Carter looked on. The state of war which had existed since Israel's birth as a modern nation was now officially over — Israel and her foremost adversary, Egypt, were at peace.

It was a fact many on both sides felt could only be a dream from which they would be rudely awakened. Sadat had, indeed, startled the world with his vow in November of 1977: "I am ready to go to the Israeli Parliament itself to discuss [peace]." Begin countered with an invitation to do just that, and on November 19th Anwar Sadat walked slowly down a line of Israeli dignitaries assembled on the tarmac at Lod shaking hands and exchanging pleasantries. One Israeli government official later recalled: "I watched it all, but I simply could not believe it was actually happening. Anwar Sadat here in Israel addressing the Knesset? It was incredible. I still pinch myself once in a while."

Sadat's reasons for seeking peace with Israel were both profound and pragmatic:

• Anwar Sadat was sick of fighting wars he knew the Arabs could not win. He recognized only too well the truth of the statement: "When the

Arabs go to war against Israel, Egyptians die." Since the rebirth of Israel, Egypt had been in the forefront of every significant military conflict. She had paid more, suffered more and lost more than any other Arab nation.

• His nation was immersed in devastating poverty which threatened the stability of his government. Sadat could no longer countenance a poverty-for-belligerence lifestyle.

• His relationship with the Soviet Union had deteriorated to a point that he expelled Russian military advisers (1972) and later renounced the Soviet-Egyptian Treaty of Friendship and Cooperation (1976). This left Egypt with a 4 billion dollar debt and no more credit from the U.S.S.R. His only other big power option was the United States. A bold move to bring peace assured solid U.S. military and economic support.

• The humiliation of losing the Sinai was compounded by the futility of attempts to regain it by military force. Negotiation was the only avenue which held any likelihood of regaining lost territory.

For his part, Jimmy Carter also believed it was a dream that could come true and invested vast amounts of his time and energy in an all-out effort to make the dream a reality. Carter convened the historic Camp David negotiations on September 5, 1978 with some basic commitments, prayer and a Bible under his arm.

"I went to Camp David with all my maps, briefing books, notes, summaries of past negotiations, and my annotated Bible, which I predicted — accurately, it turned out — would be needed in my discussions with Prime Minister Begin.

"The Judeo-Christian ethic and study of the Bible were bonds between Jews and Christians which had always been part of my life," Carter said. "I also believed very deeply that the Jews who had survived the Holocaust deserved their own nation, and that they had a right to live in peace among their neighbors. I considered this homeland for the Jews to be compatible with the teachings of the Bible, hence ordained by God. These moral and religious beliefs made my commitment to the security of Israel unshakable."

The president told Cyrus Vance: "We'll ask the religious leaders to set aside a week of special prayer." When it appeared the talks at Camp David would fail: "I remained alone in the little study where most of the negotiations had taken place. I moved over to the window and looked out on the Catoctin Mountains and prayed fervently for a few minutes that somehow we could find peace."

Carter's sense of history and destiny was shared by participants and observers as well. The leaders of nations representing the world's three major religions, Judaism, Christianity and Islam, were meeting in close

94

proximity to the Bible in an attempt to secure peace for the region of the world from which all three had come. It was indeed a time that caught the imagination and fueled the dreams of men and women around the globe. One Egyptian official saw things in millennial terms: "I envision a day when Israeli farmers will be harvesting crops in a Negev made green by the waters of the Nile."

In the midst of all of this, Israelis, who were at center stage during the negotiations, were buzzing with excitement and anticipation. When Carter and his entourage came to Israel, activities of the nation became incidental to where he was, what he was doing, and what he might say.

The Weichert family was no exception. They were accustomed, as were other Israelis, to world leaders being in the Promised Land. But this was different. Their future was being affected, and events were in the balance that held the potential of quieting at least one major battle front. Zvi was paying close attention.

For the Carters, activities would not be confined exclusively to stuffy conference rooms. They would occasionally leave their suite at the King David Hotel to enjoy the hospitality Israelis were eager to extend. Among the engagements on their itinerary was a performance by the Jerusalem municipal orchestra — Ruthi, Mendel and Yona were all members.

Music had been a part of their lives almost as long as they could remember. Their association with that art form was born of Zvi's love for music and social necessity.

When the children were small, Zvi and Esther had been concerned about there being no area where they could play except on neighborhood streets. This was not acceptable, and they spent a lot of time discussing their desire to be in a better place. But short finances squashed any serious thoughts of their doing so.

Then one day, Zvi answered a knock on the door to find a pleasant young woman who turned out to be the bearer of good news. "The city," she began, "has decided to begin a program of music instruction for children in this neighborhood. Classes in flute will begin soon. If you have children you wish to enroll, I'll tell you what you need to do."

Zvi and Esther saw this as an answer to their prayers, and when enrollment began, he was among the first in line. In their turn, Ruthi, Mendel, Yona and Eli would be livening up household activities with failed notes and impromptu concerts.

From flute they progressed to a variety of instruments. Ruthi demonstrated such proficiency in mandolin that she was offered an opportunity for further study at the conservatory in Jerusalem. She was delighted, and Zvi could

95

scarcely keep buttons on his shirt when he told friends of his daughter's accomplishments. Soon Ruth was holding classes and music clinics for her younger brothers who were, more or less, happy to have her help them along.

Her instructor, who was forced to take time off for an eye operation, once asked her to take his classes in mandolin and electric bass. At fifteen, she was accustomed to helping younger children one-on-one, but forty students at one time? That was a test, especially considering that she had never played the electric bass before. In true Weichert fashion, Ruth was up to the challenge. She did fine with the mandolin students, and her knowledge of theory for playing electric bass sufficed until a student asked for a demonstration to help correct what he was doing wrong.

"Look at me," she said to the impressionable boy in need of a helping hand. "I will teach you a valuable lesson: Every teacher you will ever have has a method of teaching. My method for electric bass is to never touch a student's instrument. You must develop your own technique. I can tell you what to do, but you are the performer. It is up to you to learn to play to your best potential." The students were impressed with their teacher's innovative instructional style and were inspired to seek their own highest level of proficiency.

By the time the Carters came to Jerusalem, Ruth was lead mandolinist for the municipal orchestra — a group comprised of the best students from various orchestras in the city. Her prize students, Mendel and Yona, were also part of the select aggregation.

Playing for dignitaries was nothing new for them. They had played in the Knesset and at the president's residence on special occasions. Teddy Kolleck, Mayor of Jerusalem, was fond of having the orchestra perform before his guests.

The Carters were to be entertained at the president's house. The president, Prime Minister Begin and other top dignitaries would be on hand to contribute their portion of dignity to the occasion. There could be no doubt about it, this was a big day in the life of Jerusalem's brightest young musicians.

Members of the orchestra were granted celebrity status by friends and neighbors. It seemed everyone wanted to find out as much as they could about what was planned and what would be played. Zvi was cool and confident that his children would play up to a standard dictated by such an auspicious occasion. Esther was not so cool. She was concerned that her children did not get out of the house with a hair out of place or one button undone. It was spit and polish in the best tradition of official functions.

At the presidential residence orchestra members sat nervously awaiting the entrance of the dignitaries. When they were assembled, the children found that they were placed very close to President Carter and the First Lady. They would have to do their very best. And so they did.

Notes flew off instruments with grace and precision. The Carters and their companions were obviously pleased with the level of expertise exhibited by the youthful group. Everything was proceeding as rehearsed when, from the corner of her eye, Ruth saw Yona's music slip from the stand and flutter to the floor. She was hit by a quick wave of light-headedness as she wondered how he would react and what it would do to the performance.

For his part, Yona was unperturbed. He was, after all, an Israeli. And Israelis, faced with a fracture of the conventional, simply take matters in hand and improvise. Stooping to pick up his music seemed, at the moment, inappropriate. He must keep on playing. So without missing a beat, he continued. There was a slight difficulty, however. He was playing, yes, but Ruth and Mendel thought they were hearing another melody coming from his direction. They were indeed! Unfortunately, Yona had not committed the piece they were playing to memory. Fortunately — or so he thought — he had an extensive repertoire of other selections to choose from, so he simply switched pieces and kept playing.

If the Carters had been pleased to this point, they were now clearly delighted. When the music ended, Mrs. Carter retrieved the fallen pages and, with a smile, handed them to the youthful innovator.

Again and again, after they returned home, Ruth and Mendel retold the story of Yona's plight and performance in the face of adversity. If Carter, Begin and Sadat were making history for the world, Yona had made some history of his own. For as long as the day at the president's house is remembered by the Weicherts and their family, they will hear the story of Yona's *concert within a concert* once more.

97

1982 — 1986

CHAPTER THIRTEEN

WE KNOW WHO YOU ARE!

J udaism's ultra-Orthodox extremists fought hard for a law they hoped would bring an end to the kind of witnessing Zvi and other believers had been doing in the land of their fathers.

They felt they had won a partial victory with passage of the "Enticement to Change of Religion" amendment in the Knesset. An outright prohibition of Christian evangelization could not be obtained under Israeli law because Jews have an inherent right to the freedom of religion.

Although Israel does not have a formal constitution, the guarantee of religious liberty was carried over from the days of the British Mandate. "Under article 15, the mandatory was required to insure complete freedom of conscience and the free exercise of all forms of worship for all."

Furthermore, in 1948 Israel signed the Universal Declaration of Human Rights adopted by the U.N. General Assembly. Article 18 of the Declaration states: "Everyone has the right to freedom of thought, conscience and religion: this right includes freedom to change his religion or belief, and freedom, either alone or in community with others and in public or private, to manifest his religion or belief in teaching, practice worship or observance."

The legislation, which we have come to know popularly as the "Anti-Missionary Law," was enacted because of the peculiar makeup of Israel's coalition government. Since the inception of statehood, no political party has been able to achieve a clear majority. Consequently, formation of a government requires participation from diverse elements who are often at odds with one another on fundamental issues. In this delicate balance, minority religious parties, such as the militant Agudat Israel (Hasidic), have exercised influence far beyond their numerical strength. These parties occupy only about ten percent of the Knesset seats at any given time. Withdrawal of their support, however, would bring down the government and force new elections.

In this scenario, bargaining and trade-offs are an ongoing fact of political life, and some legislation that is unpalatable to the great majority of Israelis must be swallowed in order to keep the government running. The "Anti-Missionary Law" is a case book study in the strong arm tactics of the ultra-Orthodox.

"Enticement to change of religion" is the essence of the amendment. What the law really says is: *You can't buy converts for your religion.* Giving "money, or another benefit" to a would-be convert can result in heavy fines or five years imprisonment.

This law does not specify discrimination against Christians or missionaries. Ostensibly, it covers all religious activities by all religions represented in Israel. But it was introduced by a rabbi with the stated objective of stopping missionaries who "ensnare souls" among the public at large or Israel's military personnel.

On the surface, it would seem that the bill would carry little weight. What serious evangelical Christian would be the least bit interested in purchasing souls? The idea is ludicrous. But extremists see it as a valuable device in harassing, threatening or otherwise intimidating believers who share their faith in Jesus as Savior and Messiah of the Jews. To be charged with being a "missionary," therefore, looms as a potentially serious accusation when unprincipled fanatics choose to use it against you.

Zvi saw the face of the process close up when a man and his son stopped him on the street not far from his home. "Zvi, wait a minute, I need to speak with you."

Zvi recognized the pair and stopped. "Yes. What can I do for you?"

The man hesitated before saying, "I think you know what I want to discuss with you."

"No, I'm afraid I don't know what you're getting at. You will have to explain."

The son spoke up. "Zvi, we know who you are."

"So you know who I am. I know you know who I am — my home is just up the street. What does you're knowing who I am have to do with our conversation?"

They didn't seem anxious to end the game there on the street, and Zvi didn't have time to waste. "Look," he suggested, "I don't have time to talk now. Why don't you come around to the house later. Then you can tell me what you want."

Later that evening, a knock on the door announced their readiness to reveal the purpose of their mission.

"Zvi, we know of the book that has been written about your life. We know who you are. We also know that you have connections with missionaries."

"Yes," Zvi replied, "I make no secret that a book has been written about my life. Furthermore, whom I choose to associate with is not something of which I am ashamed."

"Perhaps not. But if this information fell into the hands of certain authorities, you know you would be in for a great deal of trouble. It wouldn't be good for you or your family if they knew these things."

Now his visitors were approaching their point.

"I can do you a big favor by seeing to it that your secret stays with us and goes no further. In exchange, you can do us a little favor too. I am in some financial difficulty. If you will help me a little, we will forget what we know."

The cat was out of the bag. The men had their answer just as quickly.

"I will tell you," their host smiled, "if you want to do me a favor — not a little one, but a big one — go immediately and tell them. I can assure you that they already know who I am. Better yet, go to the newspaper and take out an advertisement. I will be glad to give you a picture to print, if you wish."

Obviously deflated, his visitors did not know quite what to say. Just then, Esther told them she had prepared the evening meal with the intention of their sharing it, so they sat down to eat as Zvi continued the conversation.

"We don't live in fear because we are believers in Jesus. There is nothing to hide. We live openly and talk freely of our desire for other Jews to come to know their Messiah. This is my hope for both of you. Let me tell you why."

Over the next several hours, he gave them a detailed witness for Christ and explained carefully why they, as Jews, had every reason to become believers too.

At one point in the conversation, the man stopped his host with a question. "But why do you take the time to tell us these things knowing how we feel about you and what you believe?"

"My reason is very simple. First, I have already told you why, as Jews, you have every reason to become believers. But there is another reason. It is found in the Book of Ezekiel in the Bible. Let me read it for you. 'When I say unto the wicked, Thou shalt surely die; and thou givest him not warning, nor speakest to warn the wicked from his wicked way, to save his life, the same wicked man shall die in his iniquity; but his blood will I require at thine hand. Yet if thou warn the wicked, and he turns his wickedness, nor from his wicked way, he shall die in his iniquity; but thou hast delivered thy soul' [Ezek. 3:18-19].

"If you were listening, you heard that a believer has an obligation to the Lord to try and get wicked men to turn from their sinful ways and come to Him. I feel that I also have an obligation to you, to tell you the truth and give you a chance to know the Lord. When I have done this, I have done all I can do for you. You and the Lord must do the rest."

Those solemn words silenced his visitors and seemed to give them something to think about. When they left shortly thereafter, they were empty-handed. Zvi hoped they carried away something more in their hearts than they brought when they came.

There are others in Israel who are also working hard to stop believers from sharing their faith. One group has set up offices in towns all over Israel designed to monitor missionary activities and oppose anything they interpret as an effort to help Jews find Christ.

In their view, when a Jew becomes a follower of Jesus, a Jewish soul has been lost. For a Jew to allow this to happen to another Jew is a sin of tremendous magnitude. Therefore, whatever must be done to keep it from happening is completely justified. If that means committing acts of violence, so be it.

As a means toward this end, a bill was offered in the Knesset in 1985 which read in part: "Any non-Jew, be he an Israeli citizen or not, if he ... preaches, writes, speaks, lectures, teaches or tries to influence in whatever way ... Jews to abandon their faith and accept principles contrary to Judaism," even if they do so *"of their own free will and without being solicited* [italics ours] ... will be expelled from the country ... and their citizenship will be taken away. Any person born Jewish who does one of these things ... will be sentenced to 5 years imprisonment ...."

The legislation was overwhelmingly rejected by the Knesset. The mere fact that it was introduced, however, demonstrates how serious some of Zvi's countrymen are in their quest to create a Jesusless Israel.

Their anxiety is heightened by the fact that in the aftermath of the Yom Kippur war many in Israel were beginning to seek alternatives offering personal peace and fulfillment. Some sought it in a return to Orthodox Judaism. Others pursued it through the cults. Still others found it by embracing Jesus as Messiah and Lord.

This growing shift in attitude reflects a perceptible change to be found among many second-generation Israelis, and it frightens the opponents of believers in Jesus. The post-World War II immigrants to Israel had extremely deep feelings toward anything called Christian. The Holocaust, they were convinced, was but the crowning atrocity after two thousand years of humiliation at the hands of "the Christians." Hitler's Germany was the theological center of Christendom. The people who had "processed" their loved ones through the gas chambers had been "Christians." Those in "Christian" Europe, who were not themselves actually involved as participants, ignored the stench of burning bodies and refused to help dying Jewry. And, after all, wasn't the archmaniac himself, Adolph Hitler, one of them.

This was the impetus that drove Jewish immigrants to respond with the kind of hostility Zvi had witnessed toward the Swiss woman distributing Bibles in Talpiyot immediately after the War of Independence. After he had become a believer, he too had lived perpetually against the cutting edge of their bitterness. Believers were traitors who had joined their most hated enemy — the "Christians." They had denied their own people and desecrated the memory of six million dead Jews. Worse than turncoats, they were no longer acknowledged as Jews.

That perception was, of course, terribly inaccurate and devastatingly unfortunate. True believers were much more akin to the names gracing the plaques along the Street of Righteous Gentiles at Yad Vashem. People like Corrie Ten Boom, whose name is inscribed on one of those plaques, were contradictory illustrations of the Christlike compassion of genuine believers.

And while many have labored untiringly to keep the horrors of the "Christian" Holocaust fresh in the minds of Jewish people, second-generation Israelis have seen the other side. During their lifetimes, the guns have not been held by "Christians." Muslims have been the ones who conspire to "drive the Jews into the sea." The Asaads, Nassers, Arafats, Nidals and their infamous consorts have taken aim on Israel's innocents with the intent to kill.

Christians, on the other hand, have for nearly four decades streamed into the Promised Land from Europe and North America by the millions. The message almost universally carried is one of solidarity, support and unswerving commitment to the preservation of the nation and the God-given rights of Jews in their land, Israel. The most ardent supporters of Israel in the world today are unquestionably evangelical Christians who continue to say by their presence, monetary support and encouragement: We love you!

As a result, many young Jews, in a generation that has seen nationalistic idealism reduced to a tenacious struggle for survival and a search for some semblance of purposeful meaning to life, will no longer accept the pat answers of those who want to keep them in a religious system they feel has failed them. Some are finding what they have been searching for in Jesus.

The winsomeness of good Jews, who are also loyal Israelis, living the secure, joyful and fulfilling life they have found in the Lord Jesus Christ will certainly be opposed until the Lord comes. It will never, however, be denied the power of its appeal.

Text of "Anti-Missionary" Law

ENTICEMENT TO CHANGE OF RELIGION

Giving of 'Bonuses' as Enticement to a Change of Religion:

He who gives, or promises to give money, an equivalent (of money), or other benefit in order to entice a person to change his religion, or in order to entice a person to bring about the change of another's religion, the sentence due to him is that of five years imprisonment, or a fine of IL 50,000.

Receiving of 'Bonuses' in Exchange for a Change of Religion:

He who receives, or agrees to receive money, an equivalent (of money), or a benefit in exchange for a promise to change his religion, or to bring about the change in another's religion, the sentence due to him is that of three years imprisonment, or a fine of IL 30,000.

CHAPTER FOURTEEN

THE FATHER KNOWS OUR TROUBLE

I t was different this time — really different. Israel had launched the attack on the terrorists in Lebanon. The army had been mobilized. But the men with the red cards did not come for Zvi. His duty days in the IDF had finally come to an end. It went unnoticed in the public media, but this war would be unique to the history of modern Israel. For the first time in her history, the state of Israel would go to war without Zvi Weichert in the ranks. This time around, he would sit with Esther, listen to field reports on the radio and scan the daily papers to keep abreast of developments to the north. It was not as though his presence would not be felt, however. Zvi had watched as his three sons, each in a different branch of the service, left home to fill vital roles in the perpetual struggle to keep Israel alive and free. That's what made it so very different this time.

Zvi had been going away to war all of his adult life. He knew all too well what it was like to linger for a long moment at the door, pack an automatic weapon on his back and wonder how it would be for them while he was gone. Each time their faces had told him what they were thinking: "Will we ever see him alive again?" It was a tough way for him to leave, and for them to be left behind. Now he was on the *being left* side of the scene. As it came time for each of them to go, he embraced his boys and watched them leave for their duty posts. He didn't say it, but he was experiencing the same quiet distress his departures had caused the family for so many years. It was, he thought, so much more difficult to stay than to go. If only they could be children again, and he could go for them all, he would feel much better about the whole affair.

When they had all gone and the house was quiet, Zvi saw a side of Esther she had never allowed him to see in quite the same way — a way, he was sure, she must have felt and acted when he had gone away to fight. She wouldn't sit down for long periods of time, but paced around the room giving unneeded attention to insignificant items. "Zvi," she said finally with a worried sigh, "what will we do if they don't come back? They seem like just children. What do they know of fighting and war?" To Esther, they were just children. But then, they would always be children to her — mothers are that way.

"Esther, sit down," Zvi said. "I understand how you feel. They are children to me too. But you must remember, they are not really children, they are men, men who are well-trained for their jobs in the service. They will know what to do. You mustn't worry.

"Beside, hasn't the Lord always been faithful in answering our prayers? You know we have always trusted them to Him, and He hasn't failed us. He won't fail us now." So, as they would do many times through each long day inwardly, and together in the living room every evening, Zvi and Esther prayed that the Lord would hedge the boys about with His safety and bring them home soon.

The Lord did provide the rest and assurance they sought — He always did. But still, Zvi was a father, and he didn't find much to smile about while the boys were gone. He knew war too well. And he would find his thoughts, at odd times, stealing away to the north. "I wonder where Yona and Eli are. What is Mendel doing about now?" In reality, he was a father doing a father's job — it's a father's job to be concerned for the welfare of his children. Zvi would have the opportunity to pass that lesson along to some people who needed it badly before many days had passed.

The man seemed to be very deeply depressed when Zvi noticed him waiting for the bus. As he was accustomed to doing, Zvi probed gently to see if he could offer some assistance. "Are things all right for you?" he asked.

"You ask such a question of a man who has so much trouble? No, I will tell you, things are not all right for me."

"What is wrong?"

"We are at war, and my only son is in Lebanon — I don't know where. God only knows if he is safe, and if we will see him again. At times, it is almost more than I can bear.

"And as if I didn't have enough to worry about with my boy, my wife is about to drive me crazy. She is crying day and night and asks questions I cannot answer. We end up shouting at each other almost every day. Sometimes I wonder if she will keep her sanity."

"Tell me," Zvi asked, "what does your son do in the army?"

"He drives a truck."

"Well, that should help to ease your mind. Truck driving is a very good job. There is danger, of course, but not like some things soldiers have to do."

"I've thought of that, and I'm glad his work is not more dangerous. But that doesn't seem to help much."

"Look my friend, before you is a man who is also a father. I know how you feel. But I have not one son in the army, but three. They are all away because of the war. It is bad, yes, but my wife and I have committed them to the Lord, and we have peace because they are in God's hand."

"It might be too much to ask," the man said haltingly, "but would you have time to come to my house and talk with me and my wife?"

"I will make the time. As a matter of fact, I can go with you now, if you wish."

When they arrived at the man's home, Zvi waited in the living room while he went to tell his wife they had company. "I have brought a friend home with me. Come out and meet him. We will have some coffee and talk." He spoke in muffled tones; she did not.

The woman was obviously agitated. "You know I am in no condition to have company," she shouted. "Send him away!"

Zvi was ready to leave immediately — with or without the opportunity to excuse himself. But the man was talking again, this time rather insistently. "But you don't understand. This man has three sons in the war. I want him to talk to us about Moshe."

"Oh," she said. "you go put on some water, I'll be right out."

The woman talked in quick bursts as they sipped coffee and shared cake together. "I understand you have three sons in the war. I wish you would tell me your secret for staying so calm about it all," she concluded.

"You are a mother. I can understand how you feel. Quite naturally, you are troubled over your Moshe's safety. What you need is a friend to whom you can take your trouble, one who will take it as his own.

"I have such a friend. He is the Lord. I take my boys and my troubles to Him, and He gives me peace.

"I have been thinking much about this since the war. I, like your husband, am a father. But I am a father who has seen more than his share of war. When I think about my boys, I know what they are going through — I have been there before them. So they have a father who knows their troubles. In a better way, I have a Father — the Lord — who knows my troubles. And He can go where we cannot to do for our children what no human being, not even a father or mother, can do.

"You need to learn this lesson: The Father knows our trouble."

"I've never heard it put quite that way," she said quietly. "That's a very interesting concept."

"I received it from the Bible," Zvi explained. "From Psalm 27, I learned that the Lord wanted to be my Father. 'When my father and my mother forsake me, the LORD will take me up' [Ps. 27:10].

"When I discovered this, I found also that I could ask Him, 'Teach me thy way, O LORD, and lead me in a plain path' [Ps. 27:11]. These words caused me to want to know the Lord as my Father. You can know Him as your Father too."

For over an hour, his newfound friends listened as he shared a witness with them. Thereafter, Moshe and his parents became a part of Zvi and Esther's prayer concern for those touched by the war. Zvi would learn that the boy did return safely to his home. He could only hope and continue to pray that they would turn in faith to the One who wanted to be a Father to all of them.

CHAPTER FIFTEEN

OPERATION PEACE FOR GALILEE

Z vi's words to the man and woman who were anguished over an only son in Lebanon could have been directed to the entire nation. Israel did, indeed, need "the Father who knows our troubles."

As we have seen, the Yom Kippur War helped breed the infestation which matured into the acute trauma which Lebanon became. It began with a series of savage incidents, then afflicted Israel's northern settlements and finally spread like a flame throughout the entire nation. Eventually, Lebanon became a quagmire that drained Israeli life blood, divided the nation and cast shadows reminiscent of those falling on the United States after Vietnam.

By the time Israeli Defense Forces penetrated southern Lebanon on the morning of June 6, 1982, Lebanon no longer existed as a viable national entity. It had been torn to shreds by Arab internal and external factions who had for years systematically slaughtered one another in attempts to gain control of the country. By June of 1982, the PLO had achieved their designs to create a state within the state, and Yassir Arafat and his terrorist "fighters" were doing pretty much as they pleased — a situation that provided the last straw in the destabilization of Lebanon. PLO occupation of southern Lebanon posed a threat to northern Israel which could not be ignored.

From its inception, Lebanon was a country that, by virtue of its origin and makeup, invited internal strife and the bloodletting that would eventually ravage the population. The country was created by the French in 1920 during her mandatory supervision of the region. Damascus never forgot or forgave and welcomed ensuing opportunities to intervene as a "peacemaker" when squabbles broke out. Consequently, at one time or another, Syria has sided with virtually every faction in Lebanon, and in the case of the PLO, several times. Syria's goal is clearly to annex Lebanon or at least have a puppet government permanently in place.

France granted independence to Lebanon in 1943, and a government was formed which reflected the delicate balance between various factions. Based on the last national census taken in 1936, Maronite Christians (Catholic) had the numerical advantage over Moslem and Druze nationals. Thus, the president was always a Christian, while the prime minister was chosen from the Moslem population. Other appointments were made on the basis of apportioned representation from other religious and ethnic groups. This created a delicate and predictably suspicious working arrangement among members of the governing body.

By 1970, Moslems felt they had surpassed the Christians in numbers of citizens and began agitating for change. Functionally, Lebanon consisted of family fiefdoms which controlled various areas of the nation. Gemayels, Chamouns and Franjiehs dominated the Christians; Jumblatts were chief among the Druze; Moslems (Sunni and Shiite) were segmented by a variety of family and sectarian groups. As matters deteriorated within the country, these elements turned their respective areas into armed camps.

Further complications came with the founding of the PLO and Abdul Nasser's pressuring Lebanon into granting them areas of operation beyond government control. The PLO was also granted extraterritorial rights, predominantly in the refugee camps in the south. Finally, the PLO gained what amounted to a free hand to conduct operations against Israel from Lebanon.

Following the PLO problems in Jordan (1970), when Hussein deposed and expelled the PLO — an action remembered as "Black September" — 150,000 Palestinians left Jordan and moved to Lebanon by way of Syria. About 50,000 of their number were hard-core PLO terrorists who settled in the Beruit area. Another 100,000 moved into the southern sector around Tyre and Sidon and joined another 200,000 already in the region. This placed nearly one-half million Palestinians in Lebanon, with the military arm operating out of Beruit.

A final chapter opened with the signing of the Melkart Agreement in 1973. This accord granted the PLO extended influence, beyond what had already been granted in the Cairo Agreement, and marked the formal beginning of the PLO's "mini-state."

By 1975, over twenty major private armies were operating within the country. Each had its loyalties, territorial and governmental aspirations, and saw the destiny of Lebanon resting on the shoulders of their particular leader. It was truly a prescription for disaster.

Behind it all lurked the Soviet Union and her imperialistic designs for annexation and the humiliation and subjugation of Israel. She was investing millions upon millions of dollars in weapons of war to assist her clients, mainly the PLO and Syria, in furthering her own objectives.

By the time the Israelis intervened, the morass of spheres of influence looked like this:

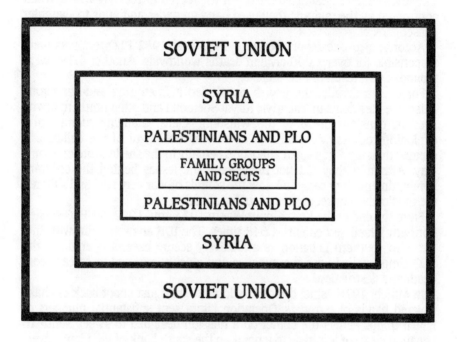

From 1970 through 1978, the PLO carried out terrorist attacks in Israel from their bases in Lebanon. Russian-made Katyusha rockets, artillery and mortar shells rained down on the settlements. The terrorists almost never directed their assaults against military targets or personnel. Almost without exception they chose helpless civilians as their targets. Elderly people and children seemed to be favorite victims. An example is the 1974 attack in Ma'alot. Twenty-four civilians, mostly children, were killed. Nearly a score more were wounded in the encounter.

Such tactics are standard procedure for the cowardly terrorists the international press insists on calling "fighters." They turn towns and cities into vast armories of weapons, complimented by antiaircraft and artillery batteries. These storage depots, gun emplacements and staff operational offices are routinely placed in schoolyards, among apartment houses in residential areas, next to churches and hospitals.

In the spring of 1978, Israelis witnessed another horror when the PLO commandeered a bus on the coastal highway near the town of Zichron Ya'acov. The terrorists forced the driver to proceed to Tel Aviv where, when confronted by the military, they used hand grenades and guns to slaughter passengers.

According to one report, between 1968 and 1982 PLO terrorists were responsible for over 1,000 civilian deaths worldwide. Another 4,250 were wounded as a result of PLO attacks.

For over a decade, the Jewish people led a frustrating and dangerous existence. Residents in Nahariya, Kiryat Shemona and other northern towns lived in constant dread of the whistling shells, thudding mortars and exploding rockets. Most difficult of all was the plight of the children. It seemed their time was spent almost perpetually in the shelters, out of harm's way. Although they did not understand the issues behind the constant bombardment, they came to know the sounds of war very well and suffered the predictable consequences of such a situation.

From the end of the Yom Kippur War in 1973 until 1982, the PLO shelled northern Israeli settlements 1,548 times. The IDF answered fire with fire, but with southern Lebanon as a relatively secure base of operations, the PLO simply rolled with the punches and quickly returned to spread more death and destruction.

In March, 1978, Israel decided to do more than just shoot back or chase isolated bands of terrorists. Operation Litani sent substantial numbers of Israeli troops across the border on a mission designed to sweep southern Lebanon clean of terrorists to a point on the south bank of the Litani River.

Yassir Arafat's civilian killers had no heart for facing Israeli regulars, and the vast majority beat a hasty retreat to the north. For three months, Israeli troops destroyed bunkers, removed PLO arms caches and ammunition dumps. Israel was determined to circumvent the PLO's ability to continue striking northern Israel from any point south of the river.

After three months, however, pressure and promises once again circumvented Israel's best interests. The United States joined the United Nations in pressing Israel to withdraw her troops. The UN agreed to provide a United Nations Interim Force (UNIFIL) to keep the peace between the Litani River and Israel's northern border.

Within two months of the arrival of UNIFIL forces in the area, the PLO decided to test their mettle. In a fight near the city of Tyre, the PLO killed

114

three UNIFIL troops and wounded ten others. Clearly the PLO was prepared to kill people in order to return to their deadly pursuits against their Israeli enemies on the other side of the fence. The UN and UNIFIL, however, were not prepared to be shot up while standing in the way of Arafat's terrorists. Within a year, Arafat had repositioned upward of 1,000 men within the UNIFIL zone, most in an area known as the Iron Triangle. While UN troops looked the other way, the PLO continued their activities against the Jews. In the event UN troops captured PLO personnel, they would escort them to PLO headquarters in Tyre and turn them over to their own people who, in turn, sent them out the back door so they could return to their terrorist activities. From June to December, 1980, sixty-nine attacks against Israel were carried out from within the territory "secured" by UNIFIL.

To add insult to injury, when frustrated IDF forces followed infiltrators back across the border, the PLO terrorists would simply surrender to UN forces. The peacekeepers would protect them from their Israeli pursuers and take them to Tyre for a repeat of the *front door back door* routine.

During UNIFIL's tenure in the "clean zone," they made no appreciable attempt to keep the PLO from restocking their military supply depots within the guaranteed area.

PLO gunners were back to their old operational intensity by the spring of 1981. From May to July, 1,230 rockets and artillery shells had swooped into twenty-six Israeli towns. By June of 1982, the PLO had initiated 290 more attacks against Israel.

PLO intentions for southern Lebanon were not restricted to indiscriminate shelling and harassment of the population. It was to be a staging area for the eventual invasion and annihilation of the state of Israel. A captured PLO document states the first phase objectives: "The Supreme Military Command decided to concentrate on the *destruction* [italics ours] ... of Kiryat Shemona, Metulla, Dan, Shaar Yeshuv and its surroundings ...." The document went on to outline objectives on various "fronts" and closed with the words: "Revolution till victory" — the occupation of Israel.

By this time, Ariel Sharon was in charge at the defense ministry, and Sharon was ready to orchestrate an intrusion into Lebanon. Although Israel's initial plan was to push the PLO back to a point twenty-five miles from the northern border and seek a peace treaty with Lebanon, it was widely believed that Sharon had his own agenda which ultimately was designed to accomplish two worthy objectives: (1) Destroy the PLO as a fighting force; and (2) wreck Arafat and the PLO as viable political operatives.

Impetus for the invasion accelerated when terrorists, one of whom turned out to be a Syrian intelligence officer, murdered the Israeli ambassador in

London, Shlomo Argov. Following Israeli retaliatory raids the next day, PLO gunners opened a twenty-four-hour barrage against Jewish settlements. At 11 a.m., June 6, 1982, the Israeli Defense Force crossed into Lebanon. "Operation Peace for Galilee" was underway.

Once they were inside Lebanon, the IDF found that the PLO was not their only problem. Their old foes, the Syrians, jumped into the fray. Consequently, the Israelis had to deal with the Syrians while rooting out the terrorists.

Predictably, the PLO did not stand to fight, and they fought poorly when they did. As Israeli forces rolled them up before their advance, PLO contingents moved north seeking sanctuary within the city limits of Beruit. The Syrians were much better at the business of war and generally fought well in spite of the hammering they took from the IDF.

The end of June found Beruit cordoned off by Israeli troops, and preparations were in progress to put the city under siege. For ten grueling weeks, the siege would go on with Arafat and his men bottled up in the city. PLO positions were honeycombed into residential areas making an all-out assault too costly from the standpoint of civilian casualties.

In the end, with the world's doves crying for Israel to spare the wolves, Arafat and PLO remnants were being escorted out of the city to be ferried to Arab host nations. There they would lick their wounds and prepare to begin the whole dreadful cycle once again.

The war in Lebanon and subsequent occupation was a costly affair for Israel. Lebanon was an unpopular war with many Israelis. For the first time in the nation's history, some young men refused army service. Another obvious factor was the rising doubt over just how much could be accomplished by direct military intervention. Much like the Yom Kippur conflict, Lebanon was another drain on the spirit and emotions of the Jewish people.

Sharon's objectives for the PLO were partially accomplished — Arafat's military arm had been mangled. Israel would have a considerable period of respite before he could begin to reassemble enough equipment to start over. Political objectives for victory over Arafat were not so clear-cut. He had been temporarily humbled and humiliated. He was down but far from being comatose. Unfortunately, Israel would be hearing from him again.

Syrian intentions were clarified by the conflict. Regardless of what they agreed to in the cease-fire arrangements, Syria had no agenda for getting out of Lebanon. Their presence in the Bekaa Valley amounts to functional annexation.

Militarily, Syria had suffered yet another whipping at the hands of the Israelis. Troop losses, dead and wounded, numbered 4,200. Three hundred thirty-four Russian-built T-62's, T-54's and T-72's, along with 140 personnel carriers, were sent to the scrap heap by the IDF. In the sky, 96 planes and helicopters were lost. Add to those figures the SAM batteries destroyed or captured (19), and they add up to an impressive illustration of fact: The Syrians were far from ready to take on the army of Israel.

The big loser in the Lebanese war, however, was a "nonparticipant." Russia emerged in the aftermath of the struggle with egg on the face and questions galore for itself and a watching world. Three areas of evidence surfaced:

Russia was humiliated: The losses quoted above were for equipment requisitioned from the Russian arsenal. American and Israeli-made tanks proved clearly superior to those fielded by Syria and their Russian sponsors. (Israel's Merkava performed extremely well.) Russian-made aircraft trailed plumes of smoke into the ground with alarming regularity. The Russian "missile canopy," which had so devastated the Israeli air force during the Yom Kippur War, was almost totally nullified by Israeli technology and was of no consequence whatever during the fighting. With disparities in the relative quality of personnel manning the equipment fully taken into account, the Soviet Union and her allies were given pause to wonder about the machines their men were pointing at the West.

Russia was shown to be an unreliable "friend": It was no secret that Yassir Arafat was a client of the Soviet Union. All of the warm bear hugs he received in Moscow, however, turned to ice when he screamed for help as a virtual hostage in Beruit. Arafat's calls to the North found the phone off the hook in the Kremlin. We can be sure that situation was not lost on other international camp followers of the Russians. For years, the United States had been gleefully held up to ridicule as a friend not to be trusted or relied upon when the crunch came. Now the "crunch" was squeezing other feet. The Soviets, "friends" were discovering, were quite capable of playing paper tiger too. Only an international press corp, inexplicably slow to point such things out to the rest of the world, helped soften the blow.

Russian intentions were exposed: The Soviets — prime arms merchant in the Middle East — poured arms and equipment into the PLO camp in astonishing quantities. Their reasons for doing so most certainly went beyond picking up some petro-dollars from Arab arms buyers.

Even seasoned military analysts were shocked at what was uncovered in Lebanon. Supplies stashed in southern Lebanon were estimated to be enough to fully equip an army of at least 100,000 troops — PLO strength was no more than 15,000-20,000.

Enormous military supply depots were discovered concealed in air-conditioned subterranean vaults dug into the sides of hills. The machine used to construct the vaults was a Russian-made digger, larger than anyone in the West had ever seen. One of these tunnels east of Sidon was as long as two football fields. The shaft was crammed to the doors with grenades, rockets, artillery shells, missiles, explosives and small arms ammunition. A single complex captured by the Israelis contained advanced Russian equipment worth 250 million dollars.

The big questions were, "Why was all of that equipment there? And who was it intended for?"

There are two explanations: (1) It was placed there awaiting the advance of Arab armies on their way to invade northern Israel; or (2) it was prepositioned for Russians, in the event they opted to send a contingency for an invasion of their own. The second option was favored by some Israeli experts. Students of Bible prophecy also come down on that side of the probability scale. They are assured, at the least, that the time will come when Russia will exercise the invasion option. Whether the plan was so imminent, one can only guess — Israel's intervention set that program back.

An indisputable certainty is that the Communists to the North will not rest on their beds until they find an opportunity to rectify the indignities inflicted in Lebanon.

The point closer to home is this: The wider ramifications of the war in Lebanon not only touched Zvi and his family in the immediate context of their experience but will affect his descendants, their nation and our world until the Lord comes.

CHAPTER SIXTEEN

"TELL MY MOTHER AND FATHER I LOVE THEM"

Uncommon valor is a common trait among those who serve in the Israeli Defense Force. Volumes written about the military campaigns fought by Israelis since the inception of statehood are filled with heroics, courage and tactical ingenuity equal to anything one reads from the pages of the Old Testament.

In the brilliant array of military luminaries Israelis have depended on for their survival, none stand taller than those wearing paratroop ensignias. Jerusalem was reunited by Mordecai Gur's 55th. In far-off Africa, Uganda's tyrannical Idi Amin and an astonished world witnessed their exploits at a place called Entebbe. Israel's "men from the sky" have paid a high price for their notoriety. Discipline, personal sacrifice and blood mark the way of those who compete to be selected as one of the chosen few. Those few tough and tenacious young men are sterling examples of the best Israel has to offer.

For as long as Eli Weichert knew he would one day serve in Israel's armed forces, he dreamed of being a member of that elite corp. And if one were to write a background prescription for the quintessential Israeli paratrooper, it couldn't be written more precisely than Eli lived it.

Very early on, he began to practice skills in how to defend the weak against hostile aggressors. Eli was four or five when he came into the house after being roughed up by some little neighborhood toughs. Uncle Nathan, who had dropped in for tea that afternoon, did a damage survey before offering some instruction in the art of self-preservation.

"Eli, listen to your Uncle Nathan. Every place you will ever go will have people who think they are tough and who want to push you around. You must learn to defend yourself — no one else can do it for you. When the bullies start to come after you, give them a good, hard whack. Remember two things: hit them first, and hit them hard!"

Nathan's intent student listened carefully to his uncle's words then asked to be excused and left the house to rejoin the boys outside. About fifteen minutes later, he was back inside. Eli sat quietly for the short interval before Zvi heard someone pounding on the door. It opened on a mother with hostile intent holding the hand of a youngster who looked somewhat the worse for wear.

"What can I do for you?" Zvi inquired diplomatically.

"You can bring that little monster out here. I've got a score to settle with him."

Zvi felt that under the circumstances, a little cool-down time was preferable to delivering his youngest son into her hand. "Just what seems to be the trouble?" he asked.

"Your boy picked a fight with my son. He didn't do anything, just said something — it was nothing — and your boy hauled off and hit him in the face. What kind of kids are you raising, anyway?"

Well, he was raising good students, that's what he was doing. Eli had decided that the quickest way to test Uncle Nathan's lesson was to put it into practice. So, at the first word of provocation, he swung into action. While Zvi attempted to take care of matters at the door, Uncle Nathan began lesson two: recognition of true belligerent intent.

That was Eli, unvarnished lover of action. He was the kid who, in family photos, always had someone assigned to his hands — keeping the pincers closed.

He was a bit older when he began attending church camps and retreats. Eli always enjoyed them for the people, activities and prizes awarded for memory work, participation, punctuality and the like. Lots of points meant lots of markers. And markers bought goodies at the camp canteen. His one problem was always conduct. They insisted on deducting points for life's little infractions. Working at point preservation was always a major project for Eli during the camping season.

He did pay attention to what was going on during worship services and from his earliest memories counted himself a believer in the Lord. He attended church, had believers as parents and lived a clean life. Although Eli was rambunctious and loved fun, he did not get involved in the "black fun" so many of his acquaintances sought after.

But it wasn't just worship services and Bible teachers who impacted his life; Eli witnessed what it meant to be a true believer every day. Esther was a model of disciplined Christian motherhood. She was always aware of the dangers of the "street" and worked at providing the constructive alternatives necessary in keeping children straight. Their after-school regimen was predictible: called in at 5:00; washed and presentable by 5:30; eating supper by 6:00; then studies followed by "off to bed" and "lights out."

Eli "saw Christ in father," and learned to adore him as a model to follow. Zvi faithfully led the family in Bible reading and devotions at home. But for Eli, it wasn't only what he said. It was something you learned to feel when you were with him. As Mendel had, he would watch him talking to friends and army buddies who stopped them on the street. He admired the easy way he talked to people in the shops, asking and answering questions.

As time passed, Eli began to realize that it wasn't enough to be the son of a believing mother and father. He had lived a good life, but good living, he knew, was not it. "Eli," he told himself one day, "you need to ask the Lord to come into your life." That conversation with himself bore eternal fruit when he sat with Marvin, a friend from the states, and talked about his feelings. He already knew the right questions — and the right answers. He had known them for a long time. Now he wanted to do the right thing. As they prayed together, Eli received the Lord as His Savior and Messiah. He was seventeen. In one more year, he would enter the service.

Eli applied to become a paratrooper and worked hard to make the grade and qualify for that select branch of the service. For him, it was not just a matter of proving he was one rugged sabra who could make it with the toughest guys in the army. No, he did it first because he was an Israeli who loved his country with all of his heart and was willing to give everything to her and for her if necessary. But beyond this, he was a believer — one who believed that serving his country was a service for his Lord. And he had something to prove. He had seen the ultra-Orthodox hide behind their black coats to stay out of the service. Others had proclaimed their religion until they became "jobniks" in the army, serving in canteens without becoming fighters.

He wanted to show them all that he was a believer, yes. But because he was a believer, he would serve the Lord in the hardest places required. Eli would show them that believers, for love of their country, were ready to fight and were willing to die for her, if called upon to do so.

Eli and his companions were excited as the time of their official swearing in approached. As with all branches of the service, the place for these ceremonies is carefully chosen to reflect the historic implications of being a defender of the state of Israel. Eli would take his oath in a ceremony held before the Western Wall in the Old City of Jerusalem. The soldiers assembled at the highest point from which the city can be entered (the gates of Jerusalem). From there they marched in quickstep toward the walls of Old Jerusalem. Once there, the route of march took them entirely around the stately walls. The place chosen for their entrance was the Lion's Gate. History leaped into the present as the young warriors passed through the gate where Gur's 55th Brigade had made their famous charge to seize the highest ground Israel could ever capture. On they went, through the narrow streets, until, as their paratrooper predecessors, they caught a glimpse of the ancient Wailing Wall — the place where Jewish tears, hopes and fears had been poured out before Jehovah for millennia.

Chills rippled along young spines and lumps came into throats as their commander began to swear allegiance, on their behalf, to the state of Israel. "I swear to the flag of Israel to be worthy to serve her and carry out faithfully all my orders in the name of my country...." Eyes were riveted on the blue and white ensign of Israel floating gently on the evening breeze. When he had finished, at a given signal, the soldiers raised their voices to shout in unison a personal pledge: "I swear!" The words echoed above the ancient walls of Old Jerusalem and seemed to linger for a moment, as if assuring their brothers and sisters that Israel's safety was in good hands.

Eli enjoyed nearly everything about life as a paratrooper. He was a young man tailor-made for soldiering, even to looking the part. The tallest of Zvi's boys, with a thick shock of black hair, Eli's rugged, tanned face and muscular body complimented perfectly the olive uniform and dark red beret he wore. He enjoyed learning military procedures, jumping out of planes, the close-knit relationships that developed among comrades dependent on one another for their very lives, and comic relief which sometimes came in scary situations.

Everybody got a big laugh over two brothers standing in the door of a troop transport during a training drop. Jump procedure called for a slap on the shoulder and a sharp command to jump. In a gesture of assurance to his apprehensive brother, one of the boys reached up, put a hand on his brother's back and started to say, "Everything will be OK." Before he could get a word out, the boy, much to the jump instructor's surprise, had leaped from the plane and was floating to the ground below. It would be some time before he would be allowed to forget his solo descent.

As a believer in the service, Eli did naturally what he had experienced while growing up at home. Sharing the Lord with other people was first a matter of simply living a Christian life before them. His comrades were well aware of the fact that he was a believer in Jesus as Messiah and that it made a difference — it was a lifestyle. When breaks from duty came and they were heading for questionable activities in town, they knew his answer to their urgings to come along before they asked. He read his Bible faithfully, and often friends would come to him with questions about religion and the things of the Lord. He was amused when a buddy came to his bunk one day as he was reading. "Eli, two years we have been together here in the army, and you haven't finished your book yet. You must be a very slow reader!"

Lebanon was, of course, inevitable for all of them. There all of the comraderey, training and pledges to serve faithfully, by life or death, would be held to the ultimate standard, combat. Eli, would come to know what his father had learned nearly forty years before him in the wheat fields of Latrun. Looking into the ashen faces of soldiers much too young to die was a long world away from training jumps and firing ranges. And when they are your friends, there is still another, more terrible dimension.

Eli's unit was bedded down close to the border between Israel and Lebanon. They had been asleep for some time when gunfire shook them rudely from their slumber. "Get down! Get down!" someone was shouting in the confusion.

There was another eruption of shooting before several helicopters swept over the scene dropping flares.

A soldier came into the tent and filled them in with as much as he himself knew at that point. "A dingy was spotted coming ashore [from the Mediterranean]; there are terrorists on the beach."

Soon they received orders to join the search. There were, they thought, as least four of them. It was urgent that they be found and dealt with before they could scatter into the darkness.

As they were forming up for a sweep through the fields approaching the beach, Eli's officer gave instructions. "Albert, you stay here and watch the jeeps. When Yitzhak comes, send him to us."

Albert, like his friend Eli, wanted to be where the center of action was at any given time. Tonight, the action was in combing the fields for terrorists. Albert didn't want to miss out. When Yitzhak came by, Albert insisted Yitzhak stand by the jeeps while he went on with the group.

Darkness enveloped them as they felt their way over the rocky terrain. They were deployed in a manner prescribed for searches of this kind under these conditions.

They didn't see the terrorist when he jumped up to fire a burst from his automatic weapon. The intruder's fire tore through the searchers and several of them went down. Having betrayed their position, the problem was settled quickly, and the Israelis concentrated on tending to wounded comrades. Eli found that Albert was among those who had been caught by the terrorist's bullets.

He was mortally wounded and laboring for a few last breaths as they gathered about him. "Tell my mother and father I love them," he said. With those few words, he was gone.

It was a scene that has been reenacted in one place or another for millennia, and it is one which will certainly pay return visits until the Lord comes to set things right. This one, perhaps made more poignant by the young soldier's parting words, was only one more reminder of the ugly monster war is.

For Eli, it was a reaffirmation of two things. He understood more than ever the absolute necessity to fight for the survival of his beloved nation. Albert did not waste his life. His was a life spent to keep Israel out of the hands of mindless maniacs who wanted to destroy them all. It was the highest investment one could make for the greater good of his country.

But he was also sure of something else. Eli was certain of the rightness of having become a believer. He was making an investment that would not be terminated when he left this earth. He was serving his country, Israel, today. He will serve in that "better country" for eternity — the one his father Abraham had looked for so long ago.

"For he looked for a city which hath foundations, whose builder and maker is God" (Heb. 11:10).

CHAPTER SEVENTEEN

IT'S A PITY HE'S NOT A JEW

Yona enjoyed his childhood. He was good looking, smart, loved
play and study and liked to keep an eye on the girls. He was aware
of the fact that there were people in the neighborhood who took issue
with the fact that they were believers. He can remember well situations
like the day he was abruptly awakened at 6:00 in the morning by some
men who had come to argue loudly with his father about their faith in
the Messiah. It was a scary experience for a small boy. But boys are boys,
and no matter what parents may tell their children about being wary of
the "Christian," when the Christian has the football or basketball, he becomes
a valuable commodity on the playing field.

At home, he felt a comfortable security with parents who showed him
a full measure of love and consistently exhibited a lifestyle that helped
shape his developing character and values. He deeply admired a mother
who could keep things together in such an orderly fashion. She was
organized and predictable. Yona liked that — it was his style too. One
never wondered about what she would say or do in given situations. Each
day, Esther was off to the market on a schedule precise enough to be the
envy of the most time-conscious airline president. When she opened the
door on her children returning from school in the evening, it was always
from the kitchen where she was involved in her most serious enterprise:
cooking for her brood. Microwave ovens and quick fix meals had no place
or sympathy within the perimeters of her base of operation, the kitchen.
She started from scratch and finished somewhere in the neighborhood of
culinary perfection. Even in the hardest of times, there was always plenty
of food on the Weichert table, food prepared with the kind of care that
showed them, three times each day, just how much their mother cared
for them.

In his private moments, when Yona thought about growing up and having his own home and family, he paid Esther the ultimate tribute by telling himself: "I want a wife who will be just like her."

He learned much by observing the way his father went about living his witness for the Lord. Oh, it wasn't a matter of sitting down in a seminar-like posture to fill notepads with "how to" information. And it wasn't walking up and down the hallways shouting, "Look at me and see a believer in Yeshua." That kind of ostentation doesn't go far in Israel. His father was often heard to say of the high pressure enthusiasts who came from abroad trying to shout Israelis into the family of God: "They bring a big wind, but very little rain." Yona learned by watching people come to their home, folk who needed a letter or document translated, or maybe they were in trouble and had learned that they could find sound advice or hands to help behind Zvi's door. And by the time they left the house, they had some word of God's love and grace to think about. In ways that were totally in the context of the conversation or situation, his father would weave in a witness for the Lord. Yona was learning, in the casual, offhand way children do, what it meant to allow the Lord to open doors for witness in a normal, Spirit-directed fashion.

To the children, Zvi was the eternal optimist. Everything they had was from the hand of God, and they could be glad. What they didn't have was in the will of God, so they could be satisfied — it was all OK! This lesson came from a man who never took the easy way around to create a "happy" situation. He worked hard at a tough job. He did it by choice, and they knew it. There was always a sense of security in this, a kind of assurance that would later help them face up to the tough jobs without fearing a loss of joy in the process.

Yona began taking his belief seriously by the time he entered high school. To this point, he had played with "good boys" from the neighborhood who stayed pretty close to his standard of behavior. Now he was thrown together with kids who were trying their wings as young adults. Discotheques, cigarettes and the like were becoming fashionable with his age group. It was at this stage that Yona began seeing what life was like on the other side of the fence. He didn't like what he saw, and he immersed himself in study and sports, areas where he excelled. Consequently, he was well thought of by teachers and respected by fellow students who knew he was different; but they also knew that he was good at what he did.

That standard held up through two years of college, and when the time came to fulfill his service commitment, Yona decided on the navy. He applied for and was accepted in officers' training school.

His choice put the men of the Weichert family in every branch of the IDF. Zvi had been regular army. Mendel was in the air force. Eli was a paratrooper. As one might expect from this kind of diversity, there was always plenty of inner-service rivalry present when the family was together.

Most people are not well-appraised of the exploits of the men of the navy. Paratroops and armored forces have dominated the public's perception of Israeli military. Indeed, until the Yom Kippur War, Israel's navy was relegated to an auxiliary role among the fighting forces. In that bitter struggle, however, the navy came into its own and outperformed all other branches of the service in overall accomplishments. This was largely due to the fact that the navy had recognized the revolutionizing impact of missiles on warfare before those in some other branches of the armed services. By the beginning of the war, Israel had built a fleet of a dozen fast missile boats. These boats were armed with missiles (the Gabriel) designed and manufactured in Israel. On the first day of the war, Israel's Gabriels blew four Syrian craft out of the water and took charge of the sea-lanes to the north. On October 10th, Israeli missile ships sunk three Egyptian ships near Port Said. Four more Syrian missile boats went to the bottom in subsequent engagements.

From that point on, Israel's navy commanded the entire coast from Syria to Egypt and raked enemy coastlines with telling effect twenty-four hours a day. Syria's coastal oil installations were ripped up by the 76 mm. naval guns. Radar stations, military complexes and supply depots in Syria and Egypt were mauled by young Israeli gunners. Egypt's northernmost SAM missile sites took a pounding from the sea.

Achievements of the Yom Kippur War led the navy into a new era which has seen the development of a highly sophisticated military arm charged with the awesome responsibility of securing Israel's vulnerable coastline from enemy states and terrorist marauders.

Those aspiring to become naval officers are treated to stiff competition and a grueling work load at the officers' school. As a numerically small branch of the IDF, the navy can afford to choose a very select group to fill the ranks. Only thirty percent of those beginning the course are around when the commissions are distributed.

Coming into the barracks dog dirty and willing to trade a meal for an hour's sleep was standard fare for the trainees. Yona's routine varied somewhat from his mates, however, and was cause for questions and some observations about this guy who was "different." Before he grabbed some sleep, he would invariably open his Bible and spend a little time perusing its pages.

"Why are you always reading your Bible?" he was asked. "I'm so tired, it's all I can do to stay awake."

"I read because I need what this Book has to say to me. As a believer, it gives me strength to go through all the things we are doing just now."

Yona's comrades knew he believed in Jesus as Messiah. But, as it was in high school, the proficiency he displayed, and the fact that they soon learned that "this is a guy you can count on," helped maintain good relationships with those about him. He smiled when he overheard a comment intended for other ears. "You know, Yona is such a good guy, it's a pity he's not a Jew!"

His friend's observation displayed the common thread among Israelis, and world Jewry for that matter, when it comes to those Jews who believe in Jesus as Israel's Messiah and their personal Savior. It was much more subtle toward Yona, but it was still a statement in the same vein as his father had experienced as a demolitions expert long years before.

"It's sad, but true," Zvi would say, "that the only time some of my own people are willing to own me as a Jew is when they find a bomb in their mailbox or trash can and need me to remove it. Any other time, because I believe in Jesus and the New Testament, I am no more a Jew."

Zvi was justly proud when his second son graduated from officers' school and received his commission. Friends and visitors to the Weichert home were given the full treatment of pictures and lectures on just how well Yona had done on his way to becoming one of the navy's officers.

For Yona, graduation marked a major transition in his life. Over all the years of his education and training, he had worked hard at the business of learning and preparation. "Now," he told himself, "the true test is coming. How will I do when it comes to putting all of this into practice?"

His concern was not limited to performance as a naval officer. He was well-trained and confident that he could do his job — at least he would give it his best shot. As a believer, he knew that he had a bigger job to do.

"All these years I've been praying that God would have His way with my life. Now it was time to see what He would do with me."

His first assignment to a ship was an experience which equalled his expectations. Going on board, meeting his commander, fellow officers and the men he would command all helped verify in his mind that this was his "element." Yona was going to do his duty to the best of his ability. In the process, he was going to enjoy his vocation.

He decided he would shoot straight about his faith from the outset, so he took his Bible into the officers' room and began doing what he had

128

done for as long as he could remember, spending time daily plying the pages of the Word of God. Yona had long puzzled over the fact that although he was among the "People of the Book" — his Jewish people — there was always a great look of surprise when he was found reading "the Book." Nobody who laid claim to being God's people seemed to have much interest in reading His Word.

Almost as quickly as he opened his Bible, he heard the now-familiar question: "Why are you reading a Bible?"

"Because," he replied, "I believe in Jesus, and Bible reading is how I come to know Him better."

"So, you believe in Jesus. Good for you." Yona was surprised to get that response. Most of the officers, he found, were men who were ready to live and let live. He was no threat to them.

Yona's belief that the real test would come when he started his duty aboard ship was a prophecy fulfilled. As an officer, he was under the scrutiny of all hands. His captain wanted to see what he was made of and how he would perform under fire. Fellow officers were concerned about their peer's quality as a leader. Yona's men wanted to know if the man behind the insignia "knew his stuff" and was worth following in battle. It was all on the line — and no one knew it better than Zvi's boy.

His first on-ship interrogator was himself, quite literally, a turncoat. The man had been raised in the yeshivahs of Mea Shearim. His biggest decision in life had come when he decided to take off his black coat, turn from ultra-Orthodox prejudices and answer his nation's call.

"So you believe in Yeshu," he said. That shortened version of Yeshua is somewhat like a curse to Hasidic Jews.

"Yes, I believe in Yeshua," Yona replied.

A curt "Why?" was the next question.

"Because I am a Jew."

"What do you mean, 'Because I am a Jew'?"

"You see," Yona explained, "if I were not a Jew, I would probably never read the Bible. But because I am a Jew, I read it. And when I began to read it, God showed me that Jesus is our Messiah."

"Where do you find Yeshu in the Bible?" he challenged.

"I will show you in Isaiah 53, in Jeremiah 31, in Micah. He is everywhere in the Bible."

His questioner listened intently as he read messianic passages to him. Immediately, in a meticulously detailed manner, the former yeshiva student began answering each verse and passage with words from the rabbis. Yona had heard the same answers many times when he was on the streets with his father. In this man's eyes, the writings of the rabbis took precedence over the Word of God. To argue was futile.

"I can get you things to read, if you are interested," Yona suggested.

"No, I think I already know the facts about this matter," his questioner said emphatically.

In the days to follow, Yona did not attempt to say more. He wanted to demonstrate, through his actions, what it meant to be a believer. He would show no favoritism, but he would exhibit the love of Christ toward the man who had no respect for his belief. Perhaps the sown seed would germinate in time.

This man turned out to be the exception among his fellow officers who tended to talk freely and, for the most part, uncritically about what Yona believed. They had respect for him, and the question of Jesus as Messiah did not seem to be the big problem. Their problem was one that is universal with people of material means. Most of these men had been raised in relatively well-to-do circumstances. Priorities were, therefore, scaled on the material side of things. Their difficulty was the same as it is for a generation of American Yuppies. Jesus encountered the same thing in Israel two millennia ago. Having so much in the here and now makes it difficult to recognize a personal need for God at all.

Yona spent a good year and a half on the ship before leaving for six more months of study. When he left his ship, he was sure he was leaving behind the best ship in the navy.

A new station meant a new commander, which also meant interviews and sessions designed to familiarize personnel with surroundings and shipmates. At the conclusion of his initial private briefing by his commander, Yona was asked if he had anything to say or if there was anything he would like to share about himself.

"Yes, there is something I feel I should tell you. It has nothing to do with the service, but I think that as my commanding officer you should know about it.

"I read the Bible, but not just the Old Testament. I believe that the New Testament is the fulfillment of the Old Testament. And I also believe that Jesus who was crucified is the Messiah of the Jewish people, but the Jewish people were not ready to accept Him."

His commander looked across the desk at his newest officer. Yona waited for his response, not knowing what to expect. "I find what you have said very interesting. Do you have more that you would like to tell me about it?"

Yona proceeded to touch on other points he felt were important to a conversation of this kind.

"But I am puzzled about something," the commander said. "If you are religious and believe in the Old Testament, why don't you wear a yarmulke and dress like other religious Jews?"

"Because, you see, Jesus came as a sacrifice for us, so we have a new covenant now, as it is written in Jeremiah 31. As a result, we are no longer living under the laws of *do* and *don't do* because God, by His grace, gave us freedom from those things. All we have to do is to accept the God of the sacrifice."

After his commander had asked a few more questions, he made a request. "If you don't mind, I would like for you to speak before the other officers on board about this.

"And while you're preparing to do this, could you also spend some time explaining just what's going on with the Mormons in Jerusalem. Everybody is talking about the big fight they are having. [The Mormons were in the process of constructing a study center in the city, and some religious Jews were raising a furor over the possibility of it becoming a launching pad for proselyting Jews.]

"Something else occurs to me. Give us some information, if you will, about the Jehovah's Witnesses."

To say the least, this was not what Yona was expecting to come out of his orientation meeting with his superior. "Yes, of course, I will be happy to do it. The only thing that I'm a little concerned about is that some of the officers might construe this to be a missionary act and try to make trouble."

"No," the man replied. "This is what's happening on the streets of Israel today. There is nothing wrong with our knowing about current events. Don't worry. There won't be a problem."

Yona went to his quarters and thought it over. So this was one of the things for which the Lord had prepared him. He was going to speak, by invitation, to his commander and nine other officers on the ship. This, he knew, was not just a casual conversation — it was a full-blown lecture. He had better be prepared to deliver the goods. He had one month to get ready. Just what did he want to say to these men who were to listen to *the hope that was within him*?

He settled on four essentials he would develop during his talk:

(1) Why, as a believer, he was still a Jew.
(2) The history of messianic hope among the Jewish people.
(3) The importance of the sacrifice to any Jewish religious system.

131

(4) How Messianic Jews who believed in Jesus separated from the main branches of Judaism.

Yona immediately began gathering source material for his lecture. He drew on friends who were well-acquainted with Jewish history and theology. He also hunted for good books and any other reliable sources he could lay hands on. By the time he was ready to speak, he had sixteen pages of information written on both sides. If he failed, it certainly would not be for lack of material. Now he faced a problem: His talk was to last for one hour. How could he possibly say all he had to say in that time?

As his talk proceeded, he managed to touch all bases he intended to cover, with special emphasis on the messianic credentials of Jesus to be found in the Old Testament.

The hour seemed to fly by in a few minutes, and as he went on, he could not help noticing that the men seemed to be hanging on every word. Time ran out as he was discussing the vital question related to Judaism's dilemma over having no sacrifice after the destruction of the second Temple. He concluded by affirming from 1 Corinthians how believers faced no such problem because "Christ, our passover, is sacrificed for us" (1 Cor. 5:7).

Questions came from every angle during the brief period given to inquiries after his talk. Among the more intriguing was one about the sacrifice of a human being being contrary to Judaism. Yona took them to the Old Testament example of God's command to sacrifice Isaac as a picture of the greater sacrifice of the Messiah. It was a stimulating and challenging exchange.

When they wrapped the session to allow the next speaker to come in and take the floor, it was evident that they were not through with Yona. "OK," he was told, "next week, you will take the time assigned to another fellow. He can wait until the week after. We want to hear more about what you have to say."

His next lecture started in the Book of Daniel and touched the ramifications of the messianic passages found there. He then moved on to the New Testament attitude toward Jewry. In black and white, he showed from Romans 11 the love of God for His people and the future promised to the nation after its coming reconciliation to the Messiah. "You can see as plain as day that the New Testament is not anti-Semitic," he told them.

Before he finished, he explained to them about Mormons and Jehovah's Witnesses — carefully pointing out the things that distinguished them from true Christianity.

When it was time for questions, one man asked, "If I wanted to become a believer, what would I have to do to get into your group?"

"It is not like getting into some secret society," Yona explained. "Everything is out in the open, and you have to decide to accept the Lord yourself. When you do, you can come to God on your own, tell Him you want to become a believer and receive Him as your Messiah.

"The wonderful thing to know is that the way to God is open to us. We can come to Him."

That night, Yona would spend some time thinking back over the events of the past couple of weeks. "How foolish we are," he thought. "I was always worried about how I would act if I ever had an opportunity like the one I have just had — if I would be able to do it. But when I did it, and the Lord was in it, there was nothing to it."

He had learned valuable lessons through these encounters. First, he learned that many people are much more open than one would tend to think. There are people who are willing to hear. Also, some people will reject your witness and send you away — as in the case of the ultra-Orthodox sailor. But if they do, so what! Among both groups are a few who really want to hear with their hearts. The worst thing is to deprive these people by not trying to speak for the Lord.

One can't help thinking of the response to Paul's witness on Mars Hill in Athens: "some mocked; and others said, We will hear thee again of this matter.... Nevertheless, certain men joined him, and believed" (Acts 17:32, 34).

Yona had taken a long stride in following in his father's footsteps.

1986 —

CHAPTER EIGHTEEN

THE VIGIL

D reary hours, which seemed to have leaden weights attached to them, drifted into days. The standard question each of Zvi's children raised on returning to the hospital was: "Is abba any better?" Each time the reply was in the negative: "No, he is still the same. Nothing has changed." Briefings from the doctors attending Zvi were equally depressing. "We don't see any change. Keep your courage up. We are hoping for the best."

A fragile form of existence was being sustained by the life support systems — not quite alive; not quite dead. It seemed as though tubes protruded from every available opening, and sensors stuck here and there on his body gave a robot-like appearance to the still form on the bed. They could only look and ask themselves how much longer things could go on this way.

Prayer was the anchor maintaining the thin line upon which their hopes hung. They were praying, believers in Israel were praying, friends in America were praying. Only the Lord could bring him back. But then, the Lord had been bringing him back to them all of their lives. In war, he had faced what appeared to be certain death many times. Was this so much different? If God could protect their father in battle, why not from this sickness?

Bedside vigils give people a lot of opportunity to talk. Things we have been too busy to take time to say can be discussed at leisure. Reminiscing about childhood, church, times — bad and good — all get a fair measure of attention. And while it is difficult to recognize at the time, or to admit later, such interludes of being reduced to the role of watchers are growing times — times when wise people stop to take stock of where they have been, where they are, and where they are going. The Weicherts did not violate these rules during their days of waiting.

This was particularly true of Ruth. She was the only daughter of Zvi and, by right of that exclusive position, had known and cherished the wonderful relationship which exists between only daughters and their beloved abbas. In the early days, he was her plaything, marvelously animated to submissively perform whatever duties her fancies would dictate. She was, at another stage, his teacher, correcting grammatical indiscretions and laboring mightily to keep him on key during family songfests.

In her mind, she was the supreme protector — the strong one — of Zvi and also the boys. But now, sitting in the hospital late at night, she was chilled by her vulnerability. Now she was the one who needed "a strong one." There was Esther, the boys and her husband, David. God had been so wonderful in bringing her such a good husband, one who was now a believer and could pray with her and help her through this time. She couldn't do without him or any of them now. But with the specter of never seeing her father again constantly in her mind, she felt that a huge part of her world was passing from her.

Like her father before her, Ruth had always asked questions. They were not always easy, and sometimes the answers produced even more perplexing queries. When she was old enough to look beyond the walls of home and church, she began to question some of the rules the family lived by. She was musical and artistic. Why couldn't she attend dances and movies with the rest of the kids in the neighborhood?

These questions were not addressed exclusively to her parents or the Christian establishment. Ruthi was asking herself some of these questions. It was something she had picked up from her father.

"All I can do for you," she could hear him say, "is tell you the right way, and show you what you should do. But I want you to learn to think for yourself and make the right choices because you *want* to make the right choices." For several years, she would have deep struggles within herself over making "the right choices."

Her desire to be like everyone else caused her to do some dabbling in the world. It was never anything bad — never "black fun" — but Ruthi was looking for the real Ruth — the person she would choose to become.

Over a period of time, she began to feel separated from the family. Oh, it was not them. They treated her as they always had. It was, rather, how she felt about them and herself. She was somehow beginning to feel like an outsider. Not that she questioned being a believer; Jesus was her Savior and she prayed to Him, but she wasn't at peace. Too many things were unsettled in her mind.

Sometimes when she was at home and everyone was taking part in discussions about the Bible and spiritual things, she felt far away from it all — a feeling not unlike the prodigal must have experienced.

As the date for her induction into the military drew near (all Israeli girls must serve two years of active duty), she began to relish thoughts of being away from home. Adventure — maybe she could drive a tank — and the excitement of being far from home were a seductive lure for the girl with a lot to learn. Best of all, she would be on her own! No more family curfews. No more house rules or inspections of new friends. Esther would not be playing "Detective Columbo" about her comings and goings. It would be great to be free!

Predictably, the freedom planned for her by the army was something far different from what she had worked out in her own mind. For Ruthi, who had never spent any appreciable time away from home, it was the rudest of awakenings.

Bedding, kit bag, towels and uniforms (which she thought must have been worn by the British) were among her first favors. Eleven girls were crammed together into the tent to which she was assigned. Her opinion of service life deteriorated further when she placed a hand gently on the shoulder of an officer to ask a question. She was barked off and told, in no uncertain terms, to keep a respectable distance. Being roused from sleep at 4:30 a.m. and strenuous calisthenics in heat so oppressive that sweat-soaked uniforms would stand on their own by day's end didn't do much to alter her initial appraisal.

It seemed like a lifetime before she could get back to Jerusalem and register her complaints at the office of the High Command. The commander was in when she arrived and listened intently as she spilled everything. Her High Commander was, of course, abba Zvi, a man who knew exactly where she was coming from.

"You must remember, Ruthi," he said softly, "you are not the first one who has gone through this. Everyone is going through exactly the same thing. Many girls in the army feel just as you do. Don't take it too hard. It will be over before too long. Try to enjoy yourself and learn from this experience." Before the talk was over, Zvi prayed for her.

She, in fact, was learning from her experiences. Ruth was passing through a personal spiritual evolution. Some lessons were coming the hard way. But she was learning.

The whole subject of suffering provides a good example of the kind of progress she was making. Often she had wondered why God allowed some people to suffer so much, while others, like herself, had experienced very little of it. She was not, she knew, better than they, but why some and not others?

Then she encountered a man who had lost three sons to the war in one day. In spite of the obvious agony he must have been feeling, he said: "I bless your name, O Lord. You know what you are doing." God was competent, she concluded. He is bigger than all of us or anything that happens to us. Ruthi began to see that God's competence could be her confidence.

So, ever so slowly, she began to get things sorted out. When the call came informing her of her father's heart attack, Ruthi came full circle. During the days of waiting in the hospital, she experienced an intimacy with the Lord in prayer she had never known before. Now she was praying with an absolute recognition that God must work a miracle if her father were to survive. Things were not in the hands of physicians; Zvi's life was in the hand of God.

Now, there in the hospital, she knew she was no longer a nominal believer who was standing in the middle, trying to keep her feet in both worlds. She was totally committed to the Lord.

—

Mendel, too, had gone through a spiritual evolution. He was an exceptionally bright young man, and as he matured it was obvious that he had the capacity to attain whatever goals he decided to set for himself. His time in the service and subsequent experience in industry demonstrated his ability as a person capable of leadership. What was now happening in the hospital sharpened the focus on what his future priorities should be.

For years, Mendel attended services because he was expected to. He was in a family of believers who went to church — it was that simple. There was no problem; he couldn't remember when he didn't believe. But there came the time when he began attending because he wanted to go. As most of us know, there is a vast difference between "expected to" and "want to."

A major adjustment in spiritual perception occurred in Mendel's life about the time he was twenty years of age. Until then, his concept of walking with the Lord had been seen as willing servitude — a sort of "bondslave of Christ" idea. There was certainly nothing wrong with that perfectly biblical understanding of what it means to give yourself to the Lord. For Mendel, it was only a matter of a missing dimension — joy in being a servant of the Lord. Those who have received the gift of eternal life in the Lord Jesus have every reason to want to present their bodies as "living sacrifices" to God. But that giving and the resulting grace living should bring a settled joy because of our acceptance by Him and the privilege of returning our lives to Him in service. Grasping these facts, or probably better, being grasped by them, had a profound influence on Mendel's life.

Another milestone was reached as a result of an experience at a party one night. It was a church function, and among the guests was a young woman who was not a believer. During the course of the evening, she approached Mendel.

"I hear these people always talking about being a believer. What does it mean to be a believer?"

He swallowed hard, thought for a moment, then answered haltingly. "I think you should speak to one of the elders about this. I can arrange it, if you like."

It was like a fist stuck deep into the pit of his stomach. He had been presented with a golden opportunity to speak for the Lord, but he wasn't able to defend his faith. The deficiency kept slamming its way back into his mind: he couldn't adequately articulate his faith in the Lord. He felt humiliated and decided then and there that it wouldn't happen again.

Mendel immediately launched a spiritual self-development program. He was in the air force at the time, and he took every spare moment to study the foundations of his faith. For eight months, he studied with the intensity of a man obsessed. Before he was through, he had produced a carefully written forty-page document which set forth his theological beliefs and personal commitment to the Lord. All of his effort quickly paid off, and he soon began to encounter opportunities to make amends for dropping the ball the first time around.

When he had finished the project, he found he had a hunger to go on — dig deeper — in Bible study. But as he was prospecting for himself, Mendel found that there were other believers who were interested in discovering treasures in the Word. Consequently, he found himself leading a Bible study for young adults and helping them in their desire to "dig deeper."

Among the people who attended the study was a young woman who was not a believer. She became deeply interested in what she was hearing and told her teacher she wanted to know more. Mendel found himself faced by a situation which was almost the exact duplication of what he experienced at the church social. But this time it would be different.

"I am working in a jewelry store in town," she told him. "Why don't you come by, and you can answer my questions and teach me more when I am not busy."

A routine was soon established with Mendel going to the store for the one-on-one studies. She, in turn, fired questions at him when business was slack. He had the answers now, and in time, it was evident that the Lord was speaking to her in a powerful way.

One afternoon, Mendel's subject was "Jesus as the Son of God." Up to this time, she had agreed with everything he had told her. Now, however, both she and her instructor friend knew that this was an issue that demanded a decision. If Jesus were truly the Son of God, and she acknowledged it to be the truth, there was only one acceptable option open: to receive Him and commit her life to the Lord.

"I cannot accept this," she said, after a long moment's reflection.

"You cannot accept what?" he asked.

"I just cannot accept what you are saying to me now."

"I am very sorry you feel that way," he replied, obviously disappointed. "But we both know this is something you must decide completely on your own. I can tell you what the Bible says; you must make the decisions related to its truths."

The girl slowly shook her head, then said, "I think it would probably be better if we didn't have any more talks on this subject."

He agreed, and the two did not get together again. But even though she refused to proceed and stopped short of faith in the Lord, there were several things Mendel could be thankful for. She had heard the truth. He had not failed the Lord or her. She understood exactly what the real issue was and what she must do about it — it was her decision to make. The Lord was working in her heart and mind. Mendel was sure he could rest in the competence of God to bring her, in His own time, to life in the Lord.

The service was another place where the opportunities persisted in coming to him. His personal routine paralleled that of his father and brothers — the Bible was in evidence wherever he was stationed. He was doing strategic and sensitive work for the air force and was firmly committed to the belief that good performance brought respect and contributed to a credible witness. Mendel had done some exceptional work in a difficult field (he won several prestigious awards for his performance) and was, as a result, held in high regard by his peers.

The consistent Bible reader became the resident expert on theology and religious matters for those in his group. A controller who came in from time to time happened to be one of the rare Hasidics to be found in the service. The man's favorite pastime was to start conversations with the soldiers about the Mishna and Gemara. "Why are you talking to me?" they would complain. "Mendel is the expert on religion. Go bust his head with your questions."

142

Mormonism was a subject that often came up, and Mendel was forced to face an old issue among Jewish people. There was the belief that because he was a believer — "Christian" — he was the same as a Mormon. Sometimes the questions almost became too much, and he would say, "But I am not a Mormon!"

This misconception rises from the situation Israelis witness in contemporary Judaism. In Israel, there are essentially three branches of Judaism: Conservative, Orthodox and ultra-Orthodox. They are somewhat different and often at odds with one another, but yet they are all a part of Judaism. From that frame of reference, it is easy to extend the concept. Christianity has many sects, so if you are called a Methodist or Mormon, conservative or cultist, what difference does it make? They are all, in spite of some differences, "Christian." This problem is among the most difficult and persistent questions raised before believers in Israel. Mendel patiently sorted out the distinctions for his confused questioners. In spite of all the good-natured digs he got about what the Mormons were doing in building their study center in Jerusalem and whether he had ties with the project, he was grateful to be God's man in the right place, at the right time, with the right answers.

—

"We have seen some improvement in your husband's condition," the doctor told Esther. "His heart seems to be stabilizing.

"I must caution you again, however, not to be too optimistic. We cannot yet interpret this as a sign of significant improvement."

Significant or not, it was a far cry from what they had come to expect from the doctor's visits to the waiting room. If it were only a small speck of improvement, it was more than they had been told they could anticipate.

More good news. "His breathing has improved considerably. If this trend continues, we will remove him from the life support system and see how he does on his own." It was like a word from Heaven! Zvi hadn't come back to them yet, but things were certainly looking up.

Then it happened. The eyes flickered, eyelids blinked open. Tears were sent streaming down their faces as, for the first time since his attack, Zvi regained consciousness. Attending physicians were amazed to see their patient rolling his head back and forth, while his eyes swept the ceiling.

"It is something we are at a loss to explain," they were told. "This is something that almost never happens — for one who has been unconscious for so long, with such severe damage to his heart, to improve like this. I can only tell you that we are not the ones who can take credit for what is happening. Someone beyond us is doing something."

But there was some bad news to temper their joy. "If this is not just a temporary phase, you cannot hope for him to be as he was mentally. Don't be surprised if he doesn't recognize any of you. We are virtually certain that his memory will be gone, and he will probably never be able to look after himself again."

When Zvi finally began to attempt conversation, it was as the doctors had warned. Mendel came close to the bed. "Abba, do you know who I am," he asked tentatively.

"Yes, I know who you are. You are an Arab!"

"Eli," Mendel said. "You come over. See if he will recognize you."

Eli walked to the bed and bent over his father. "Look at me abba. It's Eli, your son."

"Don't say you are my son. You are not my son."

They stood in stunned silence. More tears came, but not for joy. Although they had been told what to expect, it was just too much, after all they had been through, to see him like this.

Ruth and Esther sat by his bed talking about what the future held for them now.

"Well," Ruth said, "I am sure God has answered our prayers and brought him this far. If he is to be like a baby, we will take care of him. I will teach him from the beginning, just as I would a child."

She didn't have to wait long to start the lessons because Zvi started asking questions almost from the moment he awoke.

"What is that?" he asked.

"That is a door," his teacher responded.

How far they could go, or how long it would take, were two big questions. But at least he had, in some fashion, survived. They would do whatever was necessary to make the best of things.

CHAPTER NINETEEN

LAZARUS MEETS WILLIAM SHAKESPEARE

The voices sounded as though they were coming from a long way off — like echoes reverberating off corridors of stone. He couldn't figure out what they were saying; he just knew they were human sounds. But they were there, and his mind struggled to decipher their meaning.

For the first time in six days, Zvi recognized what he was seeing. It was all new to him. The last thing he remembered was standing at the bus stop on Jaffa Road. Where was he? The tubes trailing from his body answered his question at once. This was a hospital, and something serious had obviously befallen him. Like Lazarus, Zvi was beginning to emerge from the shadows.

He was in a small room — hospital personnel had moved him from the cardiac intensive care unit. On the other side of the room, he could see a woman sitting by another bed. He was thinking how far away they looked, when his eyes slid closed and he drifted off to sleep again.

It was evening when he began to reemerge into the world of consciousness. Again, he could hear voices before he opened his eyes. This time the words were not disorganized jumbles. His roommate's wife and some other people were at the man's bedside and were speaking to one another in German. Before long, Zvi could hear that he was the topic of their conversation.

"So, I see they have brought someone else to your room," the man's wife said. "I had hoped that you could be alone."

"This is not a hotel," he replied. "When you come here, you can't pick your accommodations or choose your roommates."

"Do you know who he is?" she continued.

"No, they just brought him in a short time ago. He hasn't been awake since he's been in the room. I do know he's a very sick man."

145

With some effort, Zvi lifted his head slightly and raised a hand in greeting. The man's wife turned to him and began speaking in Hebrew. Her appearance and manner told him a great deal about the occupant of the other bed and his spouse. They were upper-register Israelis. Speaking another language was "in" in certain circles where Hebrew was considered the "common" tongue of the less enlightened. In fact, Max turned out to be a person of some stature. He was a successful writer. At the moment, however, he was a man reduced to the "common" level by a common problem — a bad heart.

"May I ask what kind of work you do?" the woman inquired.

Zvi caught a condescending tone in her voice, one that didn't set well with a man who had just stood at the brink of eternity. Her question, addressed to one she had been told was "a very sick man," obviously reflected her value standards with respect to the *here* and the *hereafter*. The writer's wife did not frame her question out of a concern for his health; she was more sensitive to his status than to his state. Instinctively, Zvi saw an opportunity to give these people a few words about just how these priorities should be scaled.

"I am a carpenter by trade," he said.

"Max, did you hear? Your new roommate is a carpenter."

Max, who didn't seem to be overly interested in the conversation, grunted an acknowledgment.

Zvi had already seen the small Bible Ruth had placed on the bedside table. She thought it would help if he found his copy of the Scriptures in the same place it had always been at home. "When abba opens his eyes, I want this to be the first thing he sees."

"I would like to read something to you from the Bible," he said, thumbing through the pages until he arrived at Psalm 49. Deliberately, Zvi began to read. "For when he dieth he shall carry nothing away; his glory shall not descend after him, Though while he lived he blessed his soul; and men will praise thee, when thou doest well to thyself. He shall go to the generation of his fathers; they shall never see light. Man that is in honor, and understandeth not, is like the beasts that perish" (Ps. 49:17-20).

Zvi suspected — an appraisal which turned out to be correct — that he was addressing people who may have known much about books, philosophy and the like, but when they heard him reading from the Bible, he was taking them onto unfamiliar terrain.

"Here," he began, "the Psalmist tells us something very important, and something to which we should listen carefully. When it comes time for us to leave this world, as we all will, He will not ask us what we have done in life or whether we were important people or not. Writer or carpenter — it will mean nothing when we stand before God. Your relationship to the Lord is what will count at that time. Then you will answer for how you have invested your life — what you have done for Him and other people. This is the most important thing in life because to live here and not know the Lord is to be lost forever when you die."

His line of conversation was far removed from the levels of their interest, and there seemed to be an acute interest in changing the subject. He obliged them by beginning to carry on a conversation in German.

Max congratulated him. "You handle German very well. How long have you been in the country?"

"Nearly forty years," Zvi answered.

"It is amazing that you speak so well after being away from Europe for so long."

Their conversation was cut short when a young doctor entered making his evening rounds. He had exchanged only a few casual remarks with Zvi before he realized that his patient was no longer disoriented but seemed to be making intelligent conversation. His discovery caused an abrupt exit from the room and an equally hurried return in the company of a bevy of hospital staff members. Probing inquiries designed to test memory and reasoning ability began immediately.

Zvi returned rational answers to all of the preliminary queries. He was a little puzzled when he saw them looking at one another, exchanging astonished nods, as the questioning proceeded. When they were through, Zvi had some questions for them. And the physician in charge did a mental walk-through of all that had occurred over the past six days.

"Well, my friend," he concluded, "you have proven us all wrong. When they brought you in here, we didn't give you a chance in a million. When you regained consciousness, it was like a miracle, but we were sure you would live only as a vegetable — without a rational mind. But we are very happy that you fooled us."

"It wasn't I who fooled you," Zvi corrected. "You see, for most of my life, I have placed my trust in the Lord. I am sure if He didn't help me, I could not have survived. I know you did the best you could, and I thank you for that. But I know that it was by His hand that I have come back to where I am now. I guess we could use the old saying: 'God does the healing; the doctors get the fee!' "

That was good for a hearty laugh all around. But everyone at his bedside knew full well that there was consummate truth in those words as they reflected on what had transpired over the last few days.

No one had to tell Esther and the children whose hand was at work in bringing Zvi back to them in mind and body. They had seen a prominent TV personality come to the hospital with what appeared to be a comparatively minor problem. Within a few days, he was dead. Zvi came in clinically dead; now he was alive. It was like a dream come true — too good to be true. Suddenly, those desperate days when death seemed a certainty and the dark days after he had awakened with no memory seemed almost like they had never happened — they woke up to find everything just like it had always been. Incredibly, it was! Zvi was back on the scene with his mind operating at full throttle. Each time they came to his room, they found vintage Zvi — good humor, lots to say and eager to witness to his faith.

Several doctors were at his bedside when one of them said, "You talk about faith so much; you must be a very religious man."

"Not religious," he quickly responded. His faith was not like the religion of many who came to this hospital, which was very Orthodox in its orientation. "A man can have religion but not know God. My faith is in the Lord, not a religious system. I believe as it says in Isaiah 12:2: 'Behold, God is my salvation; I will trust, and not be afraid; for the LORD, even the LORD, is my strength and my song; he also is become my salvation.' "

One of the doctors had picked up his Bible while he was talking. "I see your Bible contains the New Testament. The faith you are talking about must be the Christian faith. It is not the belief of the Jews."

"Is it forbidden for a Jew to bring the whole Bible into this hospital?" Zvi questioned.

"No, of course, it is not strictly forbidden. But I can certainly tell you it is not well thought of by the people here."

"My friend, I can tell you that I did not receive my faith to believe in the Lord from the New Testament alone, but according to the entire Bible. If you will take the time to read Isaiah 53 and many other passages I can tell you of from the Old Testament, you will find that this is also the message of the New Testament."

"But Zvi, can you, as a Jew, really believe in the New Testament?"

"Yes, I can, and I can show you how the faith of the New Testament parallels the faith we find in the Old Testament."

He took the Bible from the young doctor's hand and turned to Hebrews 11. "Here it talks about the faith of our fathers. 'By faith Noah ... By faith Abraham ... the prophets ....' It was all by faith. Abraham offered up his son Isaac by faith. Isaac was a picture of the sacrifice to be made for us all. So it is not faith in one or the other; it is faith in the one God of both Testaments."

"You quote a lot of verses and seem to know much about the Bible. Did you go to a school and study to learn this?"

"No, I didn't learn this in school. I went to school only three years — elementary school. But when I came to the Lord, the Bible became my life. I can't tell you how many times I have read it through. I suppose you would say it is my hobby. If it is so, it is the only hobby I have in my life.

"And if you want to know why I think I have been spared from death, it can be found also in the Bible. It says in Psalm 118:17: 'I shall not die, but live, and declare the works of the LORD.' He saved my life, so I can show people the way to life."

The doctors left his room with two valuable pieces of information in hand. Professionally, they were interested in monitoring his ability to remember. Extended conversations with their patient was, of course, one way this could be done. Their talk that day provided another bit of confirmation. There could be no doubt that his faith was also perfectly intact.

Over the remainder of his stay in the hospital, they would listen intently to his conversations with the staff and get reports on talks with other patients. In the process, the Holy Spirit had a magnificent opportunity to give a clear witness for Christ.

In the end, they would be assured that his expressions of faith in Jesus as Messiah were not an evidence of a Jewish mind out of touch with reality. Quite the contrary, Jesus was reality to their cheerful patient. As lifestyle was added to verbal witness, the doctors and nurses began to develop a relationship beyond the usual patient and professional expression. They came to genuinely like the forthright man who loved his Lord.

One morning he was resting in bed when he looked across the room to find Max, the writer, reading a copy of Shakespeare's works. "Hey, Mr. Max," Zvi called cheerfully. "I see you are reading Shakespeare."

"Yes," Max thundered. "Do you know about Shakespeare?"

"Sure. He was a big writer. You also are a big writer. But even big writers sometimes don't understand the true meaning of their own words."

"And what do you mean by that?"

"I mean, Shakespeare wrote, 'To be or not to be? That is the question.' What he was talking about is not the big question. The real question is only 'To be.' "

"And how is that?" Max wanted to know.

"My Book tells us how 'to be.' And it was not written by a man like Shakespeare. My Book was written by the prophets, and they wrote by the Holy Spirit.

"The Bible tells us how to know the Lord — 'to be.' It also tells us what will become of us if we don't know the Lord — 'not to be.'

"Shakespeare had many good things to say, and we can enjoy reading them. But only the Bible can give us the true meaning of life and death."

Max was listening to what Zvi was saying, and his estimate of the "common" man was going through a transition. Even his wife was now lingering at Zvi's bed offering him generous slices of the cakes friends sent by.

It was good to see, before they separated, the writer and the carpenter sitting together discussing profound things — things as profound as eternity.

It was good also — profoundly good — to see Zvi leave the hospital to resume his life and ministry as God's man in Jerusalem.

CHAPTER TWENTY

TRINA

M endel met Ellen at church. She was a lovely girl who had come to live in Israel with her mother. Among Ellen's deepest desires was to show the Lord's love to the Chosen People. Little did she suspect when she arrived in Israel that she would become the Lord's chosen one for Zvi's eldest son.

Zvi and Esther were intrigued counselors and observers as the relationship between Ellen and Mendel progressed from friendship to being sweethearts. They were even more interested when the announcement came that the two were making wedding plans.

It was a beautiful wedding, and the happy pair settled into a home not far from where Zvi and Esther were living.

After awhile, the couple began to hear the inevitable question: "How long are you going to wait before you have your first child?" The query was, of course, of more than academic interest for Zvi and his wife, who could hardly wait. When the news finally came that Ellen was expecting, Zvi reacted with a restrained smile — he was under control. Esther began to make plans — she was going to be ready.

In due course, Mendel and Ellen presented grandfather and grandmother with a round-faced little girl bursting with good health. To Zvi and Esther, Trina was the picture of what grandparents have a way of believing they have a right to expect — the most beautiful child ever born!

When Zvi looked down into the soft face of baby Trina, he stood witness to a double miracle. God's promise of an inextinguishable posterity to Abraham is being faithfully adhered to after thousands of years. This little "seed" is proof enough. In an even more significant way, she is a sort of prophetic evidence of the Lord's promise of a spiritual "seed" in those who believe. She will be raised in the "nurture and admonition of the Lord."

And with Trina's birth, Zvi's story is no longer that of *ZVI AND THE NEXT GENERATION.* She takes us into *new generations.* Third-generation Trina is a living reminder of an eminent perfection of the ability of a faithful God to bring His people and program through. What He began in a teenage Polish Jew who found his Messiah will continue to bear fruit to the glory of God until Jesus comes again!

Mendel, his brothers, sister and others who make up the Lord's precious remnant in Israel are giving visible life and breath to this magnificent realization. Together they are bringing the message of life in the Lord Jesus Christ to the *next generations.*

These young people are taking the torch from Zvi, Davidson, Uncle Nathan and a rather illustrious band of courageous people who stood for Him in the hardest of places. They could be compared to the giant icebreakers that ponderously open the way through frozen sea-lanes so others can bring lifesaving goods and services to needy people. In Israel, God has sovereignly opened the way for a prepared people who can deliver the goods to the glory of God. And we can all rejoice in the assurance that what He began through a believing handful at the birth of the modern state of Israel will go on until that nation turns to God and calls for the Messiah.

"And I will pour upon the house of David, and upon the inhabitants of Jerusalem, the Spirit of grace and of supplications; and they shall look upon me whom they have pierced, and they shall mourn for him, as one mourneth for his only son" (Zech. 12:10).

POSTSCRIPT

When I first took up the pen to write Zvi's story a decade ago, we started in Poland with a bewildered ten-year-old boy held in the steel vise of Hitler's determination to make him just one more dead Jew. Together we have watched forty-eight years pass under that pen in recording the astounding developments that have marked his life. I don't believe any sincere and objective believer can read *ZVI* or *ZVI AND THE NEXT GENERATION* without being moved to a heightened confidence in God's competence and a deeper love and burden for the Jewish people. Speaking from my own experience, I can certainly say it has been true for me.

And if, over the years these books are circulated, this becomes an experience generally shared by readers, Zvi, the publisher, Marvin Rosenthal, and I will all be profoundly grateful — grateful because, in some measure, we will have accomplished our fundamental purpose, which was to inform, inspire and encourage readers to get involved with Israel and Jewish people.

These books, however, have been much more than charted objectives. Getting to know and love a family most of us have never met personally has been an intriguingly stimulating experience. Since I wrote *ZVI*, I seldom go anywhere without meeting readers who have volumes of questions about the man who has become an intimate personal friend to them. And knowing Zvi as I do, and having had the privilege of sharing the experience of seeing the family grow up around him, I can assure you that your affection and interest are well-placed.

They were all together when I last saw them, except for Ruth and David who make their home in Eilat. Yona and Eli were both still in uniform. Mendel and Ellen were busy getting ready to leave for the states, where he will pursue theological studies. Zvi was doing what efficient and caring grandfathers do best: observing then informing others of his grandchild's perfection. And Esther was, in her warm and wonderful way, keeping things together and all about her properly nourished.

Those of you who have met him, or read of him, and have been thus encouraged to pray for Zvi, his family and other believers in Israel, are making a thrilling and productive investment in the coming "peace of Jerusalem" (Ps. 122:6)

Jerusalem" (Ps. 122:6).